What's the Matter with the Dobsons?

Also by Hila Colman

Diary of a Frantic Kid Sister
Nobody Has to Be a Kid Forever
Tell Me No Lies

What's the Matter with the Dobsons?

by Hila Colman

CROWN PUBLISHERS, INC., NEW YORK

10 9 8 7 6 5 4 3 2 1

Library of Congress Cataloging in Publication Data
Colman, Hila.   What's the matter with the Dobsons?
Summary: The Dobson family seems to be coming apart as anger becomes
the prevailing emotion between father and daughter and husband and wife.
[1. Fathers and daughters—Fiction.   2. Family problems—Fiction]   I.
Title.   PZ7.C7Wh 1980   [Fic]   80-18980   ISBN 0-517-53409-6

For Norma Jean
with affection

❖❖❖❖❖❖❖❖❖❖❖❖❖❖❖❖❖❖❖❖❖❖❖❖❖❖❖❖❖❖❖❖❖❖

What's the Matter with the Dobsons?

❖❖❖❖❖❖❖❖❖❖❖❖❖❖❖❖❖❖❖❖❖❖❖❖❖❖❖❖❖❖❖

Chapter One

❖❖❖❖❖❖❖❖❖❖❖❖❖❖❖❖❖❖❖❖❖❖❖❖❖❖❖❖❖❖❖❖

AMANDA DOBSON STOOD BACK AND ADMIRED THE MINIA-
ture log house she had set down so carefully on the dining
room table. "It's beautiful, isn't it?" she sighed.

"I think it is," her mother said, standing beside her.

"It should be after all the weeks you spent making it,"
her younger sister, Lisa, added. "I'm glad it's finished so
you'll let me in your room again."

"Maybe I will and maybe I won't," Amanda said. She
turned to her mother. "Do you think Daddy will like it?"

"I don't see how he can help it. You did a terrific job."

"You really think so?" Her voice was nervous and eager.

"Of course I do." Kate Dobson gave her daughter a hug. "It was worth waiting for. I think you were smart not to let any of us see it until you were finished. Let's put the sheet back on so we can have an unveiling when Dad comes home."

"It looks like a dead animal with that sheet over it." Lisa turned up her nose in disgust.

"Oh, be quiet," snapped Amanda.

Leave it to her eleven-year-old sister to make her even more nervous than she was. The construction of the tiny house had in a way been Amanda's private celebration of her thirteenth birthday. On that day, several weeks earlier, she had vowed to get along better with her father: she was not going to argue with him, she was not going to let him bug her, she was going to try to please him the way Lisa did. It was then that she had decided to build a house for him. As an architect he couldn't fail to appreciate it.

Amanda didn't know why she didn't get along with her father. Her mother said it was because they were so much alike. "You're both stubborn, you both like to argue, and you both want to be right. And you're both too sensitive to criticism. If Daddy tells Lisa that her spelling is terrible she doesn't burst into tears and take it as a personal insult. And Mark is just like you. If I tell him he's wearing an old man's tie, he doesn't talk to me for a day. You're two of a kind."

Her mother was probably right, Amanda thought, but that wasn't all of it. Lisa was the real root of the problem.

She did things Amanda wouldn't be caught dead doing: she could cuddle up to their father and say ridiculous things like "You're the best daddy in the world," and if he wanted something she'd run to fetch it for him like some dumb slave. Lisa had no pride. She was little and round and soft, and their mother said that one day she would make some man a perfect wife. "Sure, a doormat," was Amanda's comment.

"You're just jealous," Lisa was fond of saying and Amanda knew she was absolutely right. With all of Lisa's kittenish, silly ways, she knew exactly what she was doing. Lisa could wheedle anything out of their father. Amanda didn't know which of them annoyed her more, Lisa for playing up to him or her father for being such a sap and falling for it every time.

"Daddy's here now," Lisa said, and of course she was the first to run to the door and jump into his open arms. "Come into the dining room. Amanda has a surprise for you."

Amanda was kissing their grandmother, who had come in with Mr. Dobson, but she quickly shot Lisa a warning look that said, "You stay out of this."

Mr. Dobson kissed his wife, hung up his hat and coat, and followed his wife and mother into the large kitchen where the family usually gathered and ate their meals.

"What's going on?" "Is there a surprise for me?"

"It's not a surprise anymore," Amanda said glumly.

"Come on, whatever's in the dining room is still there, isn't it? Can I go and look?"

"All right," Amanda agreed, and led the way. The others followed her and when they were gathered around the table, she pulled away the sheet to reveal her small house. She had built it like a doll house with no front wall so that the miniature rooms were exposed. There was a downstairs and an upstairs, with a dining room, a living room and a kitchen on the first floor and two bedrooms and a bathroom on the second. The rooms were sparsely furnished but there were rugs on the floors and tiny pictures on the walls, a fireplace in the living room and the proper appliances in the kitchen.

"It's wonderful!" The girls' grandmother, Margo Dobson, bent down to examine Amanda's creation. "It's perfect the way you put in every detail. I don't know how you did it. I guess you inherited your talent from your father and you'll grow up to be a perfectionist like him."

Amanda flashed her grandmother a smile, but her eyes were on her father. He was walking around the table examining the house from all sides. She watched him anxiously.

"It's terrific, isn't it?" her mother asked.

"She did a good job, but a perfectionist? I'm not so sure about that." Mr. Dobson bent down, peering into the second floor. He straightened up and smiled at Amanda. "I don't think I'd like sleeping in that bed too well. You didn't use a level for your floors, did you?"

"What's a level?" Amanda chewed at a ragged nail nervously.

"Come on, you've seen me use one a hundred times. When I built your bookcase I used a level so the shelves would be straight. A little glass thing with a bubble in the middle that shows if something is level. I showed it to you then."

"Oh, that. No, I didn't use it. I wouldn't even know where it is."

"I think you do know, but that's not important. You did a good job, Amanda, but there are half a dozen things that could easily be improved. The floor, for example. We could start by taking it out and . . ."

"I don't want to take the floor out," Amanda cried. "I don't want to be a perfectionist! You never like anything I do, no matter what. You just like to criticize, to pick on me." She took a tissue out of her pocket and blew her nose furiously. "You make me feel like a failure."

They stood glaring at each other. "Don't be foolish," he said finally. He took his pipe out of his pocket and filled it with deliberate slowness. "It's clear you don't want to learn from me." His voice was cold. "I thought your interest in architecture was serious, that you wanted a career, but I guess you've given up on the idea."

"Mark, she's only thirteen," Amanda's mother said. "Don't write her off yet."

"I'm only trying to help her," Mr. Dobson said. He ran

a strong, well-shaped hand through his dark hair.

"Some help," Amanda mumbled. She stooped to straighten a chair in the little house. "You don't care beans about me. You think I did a lousy job, don't you?" With a sweep of her arm she knocked her house off the dining room table and onto the floor, where it lay in a heap.

"Amanda, why did you do that?" Her mother looked uncertainly at the pieces on the floor, as if wondering whether to pick them up. Then she reached out to touch Amanda.

"Because it was no good. He said it was no good." As Amanda ran from the room she could hear her father say, "I never said it was no good. You can't tell that girl anything . . ."

And her mother's answer, "She worked so hard on it . . ."

Upstairs in her room Amanda sat at her desk and stared at the pile of books in front of her. She had a lot of homework but it was the last thing in the world she felt like doing. Instead, she picked out a record and put it on her stereo, defiantly turning it up as loud as possible. Let her father come upstairs and bawl her out, she didn't care.

He didn't really love her, so it didn't matter what she did. He was critical of her in a way he wasn't of Lisa. "You're older, I expect more of you," he said to her often, but Amanda knew better. Lisa was the cute one; boys were already on the phone for her more than they were for Amanda. Lisa had dark, curly hair and was small-boned and pretty like her mother, while Amanda was tall like her father, straight and flat as a boy; her nightly examinations could barely detect any sign of a bosom.

Amanda got up from her desk and walked over to her bureau and stared at herself in the mirror. She didn't think she was *so* bad-looking. Her hair was brown, not a beautiful jet black like Lisa's, but it was shiny and fell around her face softly. Her mouth was a little large, but her blue-gray eyes were okay and her eyebrows and eyelashes were so dark that her mother said she'd never have to use mascara. She didn't think her father hated her because she was ugly. She wasn't even sure that he really hated her—it could be only that he loved Lisa so much that he had nothing left for her. Her mother had once said that some men loved only one woman in a lifetime, and maybe some fathers could love only one daughter.

Amanda turned down the stereo and sat down at her desk. A moment later she heard her father coming up the stairs. He gave a short knock on her door and walked in. "Am I interrupting your homework?" he asked pleasantly.

"No." She shook her head.

He sat down in her one armchair and looked at her thoughtfully.

"Maybe I was tough on you, Amanda, but I honestly thought I could help you. You and your mother don't seem to think so, but I consider thirteen quite grown up.

By now you should be able to take criticism, want to do things right . . ."

"If I'm so grown up, why don't you let me stay out after eleven?" Amanda thought this was a reasonable question, but when she saw a flicker of annoyance cross his face she realized she was wrong. That was the trouble: when she thought she was asking for something reasonable he put her down. She felt a familiar knot of disappointment and resentment growing in her stomach.

"That's altogether different," he said. "There are good reasons for your curfew and you know it. I don't want to get into an argument about it, either." He paused. "I'm particularly sorry about tonight because you weren't the only one with a surprise. I had planned one for you." He relit his pipe.

"Oh," was all she said, determined to keep her cool.

"Don't you want to know what it is?"

"Okay." Her stomach muscles tightened as he frowned.

"You don't sound very enthusiastic," he began, and then gestured for her not to interrupt. "I have to go up to Boston next weekend on business and I thought you might like to come along. There are some beautiful old buildings there, and a lot of very interesting restoration work has been going on. I hear Quincy Market is really worth seeing."

Amanda looked at the calendar hanging above her desk. "You mean this Saturday or a week from Saturday?"

"This coming Saturday. Except we'd probably go up on Friday afternoon."

"Oh, no," she said apprehensively. "I can't go this weekend. Thanks for asking me, though."

"What do you mean, you can't go?"

"Because I have a basketball game and a party afterward. It's all planned."

"All planned! You can get out of it. I'm asking you to come away for the whole weekend. A chance like this doesn't come up very often."

"I know, Daddy, but I can't. I'm on the team and it's a really important game . . ."

"Don't you have substitutes? Every team does. And it wouldn't hurt you to miss a game for once. Honestly, Amanda, you complain about the way I criticize you, but did you ever think of my side of things? I offer to help you with your house, I offer to take you away for the weekend, and all I get is a big no and a grouchy face. God save me from teenagers!" He stood up. "I'll be damned if I ever ask you to go anywhere again." With that he slammed out of the room.

Amanda slumped down into her chair and stared at the calendar on her wall mournfully. He didn't understand, he didn't understand at all. She tried to concentrate on what her grandmother had told her about him. "Mark has a short fuse, he loses his temper because he gets hurt easily, the way you do. But you shouldn't take it seriously. Five minutes later he's sorry, even if he doesn't say so."

But, Amanda thought, he never flies off the handle at Lisa. Of course Lisa would have thrown her arms around him and said how wonderful it was to go to Boston with him. She'd have broken any date. Damn it, here she was acting grown up and responsible about her commitments and he got mad. What was the use? She could never please him.

Amanda gave up fighting her tears, put her head down on her desk and wept.

Downstairs in the living room, Lisa had finished her homework and was watching television with her mother and grandmother. In the last few minutes their conversation had gotten more interesting than the program she was watching.

"I worry about Amanda," said her mother. "She's so jumpy with Mark. And, as you know, he's not the most patient man in the world. They're at each other constantly."

"It's a hard time for Amanda. Most adolescents have to rebel against somebody, and I guess she's picked Mark."

"And he can't stand it." Kate sighed, her face anxious. "At least Amanda has me to confide in. We're very close."

"You sure are," noted Lisa. "You two are always having secrets. I don't think it's very nice."

"Why isn't it nice?" Her mother gave her an indulgent pat and a smile.

Lisa wriggled away. "You think it's nothing. But you

tell me not to have secrets with my friends."

"We don't have secrets. Amanda just has things she needs to talk about." Lisa moved a little farther away, scowling.

"Lisa," said her mother, "Amanda's going through a difficult period. Maybe she needs more help than you do right now." She stretched her hand out to Lisa, but Lisa ignored it.

"I don't need *any* help," she said, and then wished that she had let her mother hug her.

A few minutes later, Mark joined them. Lisa ran over to his big chair and snuggled against him.

"Daddy's girl," Kate Dobson murmured, and exchanged a quick glance with her mother-in-law.

"You bet," Mark said brightly. "Baby, I'm going to take you up to Boston with me this weekend. How about that?"

Lisa opened her eyes wide. "Honest? Oh, Daddy, that's super." She threw her arms around him.

"Now, that's a response I like to get." He disentangled himself gently so that he could light his pipe.

"Is Amanda coming too?" Lisa asked anxiously.

"No, she turned me down flat. She prefers a basketball game."

"Basketball games are very important to Amanda," Kate said. "You can't blame her for wanting to play. She's on the team."

"We'll have a good time, won't we?" Mark asked Lisa.

" 'Course," said Lisa. "When do we leave?"

"Friday afternoon. You may have to come home from school at lunchtime. I'll check the train schedule."

"I don't care if I don't go to school at all on Friday! Oh, I'm so excited!"

Mark looked over Lisa's head at his wife. "I assume this is all right with you?"

"Why should I object?"

He hesitated a moment before answering. "No reason."

"I think you hurt Amanda's feelings tonight. You shouldn't have been so critical of her little house," Kate said.

"Maybe she hurt my feelings preferring a basketball game to a weekend with her old man. I had thought it might be good for the two of us to spend some time alone." He shrugged. "It didn't work."

"You're the father, it's up to you to make it work," Kate said wearily.

"Amanda's not a baby. She knows what she's doing. And I don't want to talk about it anymore."

"Big Boss speaks," Kate said under her breath. She stood up. "Time for you to go to bed, Lisa. That is, if your father will allow it."

"Just what do you mean?" Mark asked.

"I mean you're spoiling Lisa and being beastly to Amanda, that's what," she said fiercely. "It was supposed to be a lovely evening with your mother here and Amanda's surprise . . . but nothing ever works right in this family." She turned away and left the room.

12 ◆

"Do I have to go to bed now?" Lisa asked.

"I guess so, sweetie." Mark lifted her from his lap and stood up. "I'll take you home in a few minutes," he told his mother.

"You don't have to." Margo Dobson stood up too. She was a tall woman with a straight, slim figure that belied her sixty-odd years. "I'll walk home." She rested her hand for a moment on her son's shoulder. "It's not easy having two adolescent daughters."

Mark smiled wanly. "You're telling me."

"They're complicated, but they're all terrific, darling, each one of them. Don't forget that."

"I know, I know." He walked outside with her. It was a crisp autumn night and the small Connecticut village was quiet.

"I'll walk you part way," he said, taking her arm. They ambled slowly toward Mrs. Dobson's cottage where she had lived since her husband's death three years ago. "Was Kate right?" Mark asked. "Am I spoiling Lisa and being mean to Amanda?"

"I don't know. Sometimes you do seem to pick on Amanda. And cuddle Lisa."

"Lisa's so affectionate compared to Amanda." He sighed. "Sometimes I think Amanda really hates me. Every time I try to get near her, she slaps me down." They walked in silence for a few minutes.

"They won't be adolescents forever," his mother said, patting his hand. "This too will pass."

"Maybe . . ." Mark said. "But it's not just the girls," he

added. "It's what happens between Kate and me. She and Amanda seem to be on one side and Lisa and me on another. We're not a family anymore. If anything happened between Kate and me . . . I get sick thinking about it . . . A lot of our friends are getting divorced."

"Don't let it happen," his mother said sharply.

They stopped in front of her house. Mark gave her a weak smile and kissed her goodnight. "It's not just me, Mom. There are four of us. We're all hurting."

Later that night, Amanda turned on her small bedside lamp and reached into her bottom drawer for her journal. Next to the real gold and garnet earrings she had gotten when she was twelve, it was her most precious possession. She set the much-handled, lined notebook on her knees and began to write.

Everyone is asleep except me. I'm too nervous. I'm wide awake. A big blow-up with Daddy tonight. I don't know why I made that stupid house for him, all he did was criticize it. I'm not exaggerating (maybe only a little) but he never says anything nice to me. I guess I could have skipped the game, and gone to Boston with him, but it's too late now. He didn't waste any time asking Lisa—if he hadn't been in such a hurry I could have tried to get someone to sub for me but he got so mad right away I didn't have a chance, and then he got me mad. No one gets me as mad as he does. If Lisa was different she'd have said no because he asked me first. But not Lisa—she'll say yes to anything he asks her. I try to get along with *him, but nothing works. I <u>can't</u> be like Lisa, and being me seems to bother him. I don't know what to do.*

I'm going to try to go to sleep. Goodnight.

Chapter Two

❖❖❖❖❖❖❖❖❖❖❖❖❖❖❖❖❖❖❖❖❖❖❖❖❖❖❖❖❖❖❖❖❖

LATE SATURDAY AFTERNOON LISA SAT IN THE LOBBY OF the Copley-Plaza Hotel in Boston. Her father had left to keep a business appointment, saying he would be gone an hour or two. Lisa had gotten tired of reading her book in her room and had come downstairs. For a while it was interesting to watch the people passing through the lobby, but soon that got boring too.

She wondered what her mother and Amanda were doing back home. Were they going shopping or out to eat? Why they spent so much time together was beyond Lisa. Ever since Amanda had started having her period, and then turned thirteen, it seemed as if she was always confiding in their mother. When their mother said she wished Lisa would confide in her too, Lisa could never think of anything to say. "You and Amanda are different," Kate had explained recently. "Amanda likes to talk things out. She really needs to tell someone about her problems. You like to keep things to yourself. Don't try to be like Amanda, just be yourself."

Lisa wasn't at all sure what being herself meant, but she did know she felt she was missing something at home. Coming to Boston with her father had seemed like a great idea at first, but now that she was here, she kept wondering what Amanda and their mother were talking about. When she got back they would have even more secrets together, she thought unhappily. Lisa was sure that when she and Amanda were younger the whole family spent more time together; she wished it could be that way again. So much of the time she felt lonely—Amanda hardly ever talked to her, her mother was either doing her real estate work or resting or talking with Amanda, and their father was away all day. Even when he was home and fussing over her it didn't help. It just made Amanda laugh at her and call her "Daddy's baby."

Lisa was thinking so hard that it took her a while to notice the boy sitting near her. He seemed quite old, at least fourteen, and he was very handsome. His rather long hair was blond and he was sharply dressed in a navy blazer with a shirt and tie.

When she looked at him, he smiled at her. Lisa was

flustered but she didn't want to be impolite so she smiled back. That seemed to be what he was waiting for; he came right over and sat down beside her. "Are you staying here?" he asked.

"Just for the weekend."

"I've got to stay for a few weeks. It's boring."

"That's what I was thinking. And I've only been here since yesterday. There's nothing to do when you stay in a hotel. I mean when you haven't got your own things. I miss my cat."

"I'm used to hotels. I've lived in them a lot. My mother's a concert pianist and sometimes when she goes on tour I have to go with her."

"Don't you go to school?" Lisa smoothed her skirt, glad she was wearing her good clothes.

"Sometimes. I went in Switzerland last year when my mother was touring Europe. After that I had a tutor. Now my uncle, my mother's brother, is traveling with us, and he gives me assignments. He's pretty easy."

"Gee, it must be fun to travel around so much. Do you like it?"

"It's okay. Say, do you want to go out for a soda? My mother says every place in America is overheated. It makes me thirsty."

"I'll have to go upstairs and get my coat." Lisa wondered briefly if her father would mind, and then decided not to worry about it.

"Me too. I'll meet you down here in five minutes.

There's an ice cream place right near here."

Lisa was excited. Wait till she told Amanda that she had gone out with someone who had been to Europe and was at least fourteen years old, maybe even fifteen! Some of the boys Amanda went with weren't even thirteen yet, and none of them had ever been to Europe, or worn a signet ring! Now when Amanda and her mother did their whispering about Tampax and menstruating and stuff like that she wouldn't feel like a dumb baby who didn't know anything.

Walter (even his name was distinguished, Walter Van Arken, Jr.) was waiting for her when she came downstairs. They went outside and walked a few blocks to the ice cream place. When they sat down at a small round table on cute, wrought-iron chairs, Lisa thought this was the most exciting thing that had ever happened to her. They both decided against sodas and ordered hot fudge sundaes with sprinkles on top instead.

Lisa found she wasn't shy with Walter at all. She told him about Blue Hills, where she lived, and all about school, and even a little bit about her sister Amanda. Walter had no brothers or sisters but he said he didn't mind because traveling around so much he always had new friends. One time he looked at her kind of steadily and said she had pretty eyes and the longest eyelashes he had ever seen. He asked her if she had a lot of boy friends.

"Not really," Lisa said, "I'm too young to date." She was sorry she'd said that because when she told him she was only eleven he looked disappointed. He wasn't quite fourteen, he said, and then admitted he wasn't going to be fourteen for seven months.

"I don't mind that you're only eleven," he said gallantly. "You look much older." She was sitting up straight in her chair, and he glanced at her figure in a way that made her feel uncomfortable. When she got home she was going to insist that her mother get her a bra.

After they finished their sundaes, Lisa didn't know if she was supposed to pay for hers or not. But the waitress handed Walter the check and he took it to the cashier in a grown-up way, the same way her father did, so she thanked him for the ice cream and hoped she was doing the right thing. Besides, she realized, she didn't have any money with her.

They walked around for a while in the twilight and looked in the shop windows. They both giggled when a woman walking by said to her companion, "Look at those two kids, aren't they adorable?"

It was nighttime dark when Lisa said that she had better get back to the hotel because her father would probably be looking for her. Reluctantly they turned back.

"Can we meet tomorrow morning?" Walter asked. "My mother will be rehearsing again."

"I'd love to, but I'll have to ask my father. He may have some plans."

Walter looked disappointed. "I'll phone your room in the morning," he said. Lisa thought he acted terribly grown-up. Probably from traveling around Europe so much. He wasn't the least bit like the boys she knew in school.

Lisa was not at all prepared for the reception they got when they entered the hotel lobby. The chief bellhop, a security officer and a small group of people were gathered around the front desk, and her father was at the desk speaking on the telephone. His collar was open and his tie hung loose, as if he'd been sweating. He hung up the minute he saw her.

"Where in God's name have you been? I've just had the police on the phone to send out an alarm for you! We've been searching this hotel inside out!" Then he noticed Walter. "Who's this?"

"This is my friend Walter. We went out for ice cream."

One of the bystanders, a distinguished-looking man with a gray beard, laughed. "They went out for ice cream. Kids. Her father's been tearing his hair out . . ."

"It's not funny," Mr. Dobson said sharply. "Come on," he said, grabbing Lisa by the arm, "I'll talk to you upstairs." He turned to Walter. "I don't know who you are but if I ever see you again it's going to be too soon." Then he nodded to the security man and the bellhop. "I'm sorry my daughter gave you so much trouble, and thank you very much for all your help." He marched Lisa to the elevator and they rode upstairs in silence.

By the time they walked into their room, Lisa was crying softly.

"You gave me one hell of a bad time," her father said angrily. "How could you do such a thing? Just disappear like that?"

"You didn't have to be so mean to my friend Walter," Lisa sobbed. "He didn't do anything. He's the nicest boy I've ever met."

"I don't give a damn about your friend Walter. Stop sniffling and answer me. What went on in your head that you could just walk off like that, without even leaving a note?"

"I didn't think of it," Lisa sniffled. "I didn't even know what time it was. I didn't know when you'd be back."

"You didn't bother to know anything. Didn't it occur to you that your father might be worried about you?" He shook his head in despair. "I should really give you a good spanking, but I suppose you're too old for that."

Lisa couldn't stop her sobbing. "I wish I hadn't come. I wish I'd stayed home with Mommy and Amanda. Mommy wouldn't have been so mean to Walter."

"How do you know what Mommy would have done? Well, you're here now so you may as well make the most of it. Come on." He put out his arms to her and hesitantly she let herself be folded in them. "Let's not spoil the rest of our visit. Cheer up. We'll go out and have a good dinner and see what there is to do this evening. Okay?"

"Okay," Lisa said, wondering if Walter would call her in the morning and what would happen if he did.

It was not until Lisa had eaten her last clam, one of her

favorite foods, that she got up the courage to ask, "Can I see Walter tomorrow?"

"Walter? Who's Walter?"

"That boy I met. The one who took me for ice cream." How could her father forget the handsomest boy in Boston?

"Certainly not! You're not going to spend time with some kid who picked you up in a hotel lobby. I don't know who he is or anything about him. You were very foolish, Lisa, and you're certainly not going to see him again."

"He said he'd call me in the morning."

"He did, did he? Well, he's got a surprise coming to him. I'll tell him a thing or two! If he has any sense he won't call you, not after what I told him in the lobby."

The thought that she might never hear from Walter again, or see him, made Lisa feel very forlorn. Even the elaborate chocolate dessert her father ordered for her failed to cheer her up.

"Don't look so gloomy," he said.

Lisa didn't answer. She *felt* gloomy, and sitting in a restaurant with her father was boring.

When she got into bed in her hotel room, Lisa started thinking about Amanda and her party back home. No boy as good looking as Walter would be there, she knew that. She could just imagine Amanda's face if Walter ever came to see her in Blue Hills. Amanda would never call her "Daddy's baby" again.

Back at home Amanda was not having a very good time. The basketball game had been okay, and their team had won, but the party afterward wasn't much fun: the one boy she liked was staying away from her. His name was Randy Smyrski, and he had thick black hair and a beautiful smile. He was a good ballplayer too—there was something really graceful about the way he moved. Amanda had been thinking about him a lot lately.

She stationed herself against a wall so she could watch him dance. Once or twice she caught him looking in her direction, but then he looked away quickly and so did she. It was frustrating. When Joel Cohen, who was a grade behind her, asked her to dance, she refused. The second time he asked she said no so vehemently that he blushed, and then Amanda felt terrible. She was glad when the party was finally over and her friend Barbara's father came to take them home.

"How was it?" asked her mother, who was sitting in the kitchen drinking a cup of tea.

"It was okay." She hadn't eaten much at the party but now she was hungry and fixed herself a bowl of cereal.

"You don't sound as if you had a very good time."

"I didn't."

"Anything special happen?"

"Nope." She ate her cereal in silence. Then she turned to her mother. "How do you get boys to like you?"

"You mean a special boy or boys in general?"

"Maybe a special boy."

"How do you know he doesn't?"

"He doesn't pay any attention to me."

"Maybe he's shy. Boys are sometimes shyer than girls."

"He's not shy. He fools around with everyone else. There's something about me he doesn't like. I can tell."

"Nonsense. Your trouble is you put yourself down too much."

"That's because I'm a nothing. I'm not pretty like Lisa, and I can never think of witty, funny things to say. Even my own father thinks I'm stupid."

"Forget what your father says." Her mother's voice was so sharp that it startled Amanda. "He's confused about women," she continued. "He wants them to be docile and sweet and independent all at the same time. He doesn't know how to deal with you when you stand up to him, and yet I think he admires it too."

"He sure doesn't show it."

"I know," her mother sighed. "It's very hard."

"Do you love Daddy?" Amanda asked, suddenly feeling very anxious.

Her mother didn't answer right away. Finally she said, "Yes, I guess I do love him. But we have been fighting an awful lot lately. This weekend was a mistake—him and Lisa and you and me. Our family pairs off that way too often."

"Why didn't you go up to Boston with him?"

"He didn't ask me. I honestly think it just never occurred to him."

Amanda was surprised. "Don't you mind?"

Kate put her teacup in the sink. "I guess I do, but . . ." she faltered.

Amanda stood and put her arms around her mother. "I love you, Mommy."

"I know. I love you too."

Amanda kissed her mother goodnight and went up to bed feeling uneasy. She was too tired to write much in her journal but she did manage to scrawl a couple of sentences:

I thought this was going to be a fantastic weekend without Daddy and Lisa, but it's gone flat. I don't know why—it's not that I miss them, it's a relief not to have them around. But I'm scared. Mommy seems so unhappy. Even though there's a lot of fighting I'd die if Mommy and Daddy got divorced. But maybe not. I'd live alone with Mommy and Lisa could live with Daddy. Everybody might be better off that way. I wonder if Daddy would even miss me . . .

Chapter Three

❖❖❖❖❖❖❖❖❖❖❖❖❖❖❖❖❖❖❖❖❖❖❖❖❖❖❖❖❖❖❖❖❖❖

A FEW WEEKS LATER LISA AND AMANDA WERE UPSTAIRS IN bed, but neither one was asleep. Lisa had her letter from Walter Van Arken, Jr., under her pillow; its ink was streaked with tears. In the next room, Amanda was staring into the darkness with mixed feelings. She felt sorry for Lisa but she was thinking hard about the words her mother had yelled at her father earlier that evening: "We all know Lisa's your favorite, it's no secret. But I never thought you'd be so childish. Can't you see what you're doing to Amanda? You act as if you don't care about anyone but Lisa."

Downstairs her parents were still quarreling, and they weren't even trying to keep their voices down.

"You're jealous of that boy, that's why you don't want Lisa to see him. You're ashamed to say so," accused their mother.

"That's the most ridiculous thing I ever heard. We don't know anything about him. I'm not going to let her go to New York to meet a stranger."

"Poppycock. We do know enough about him. *I* know who his mother is even if you don't. She's a well-known pianist. He wrote Lisa a perfectly nice letter inviting her to lunch and a matinee. She'd be home for dinner. What do you think he's going to do, rape her?"

"That's a lousy thing to say! Anyway, what about you and Amanda? You let that girl get away with murder. She's sloppy with her work, she gets terrible marks in math and you keep telling her she's wonderful. She's getting to be a stuck-up fresh kid."

"Stuck-up! That just shows how little you know. That girl has no sense of herself at all. She doesn't even think she's pretty because of the way *you* put her down all the time. She needs someone to give her confidence and God knows you don't do it."

"I'm honest with her, that's all. I don't feed her a lot of baloney. She can't take any criticism—that's her problem."

"You don't just criticize, you pick and pick on her. But we've gotten away from the subject. Are you still not going to let Lisa go to New York to meet that boy?"

"I'm not. She's far too young to go out on a date. And that's that."

"Well, you'll have to tell her. You make these decisions and then expect me to do the dirty work. No more. You explain to Lisa why she can't go. You haven't given me one good reason; maybe you can dream one up for her."

"You just don't want to hear my reasons."

"I've heard enough. Goodnight, I'm going to bed."

Amanda heard their mother coming up the stairs and put her head under the covers, pretending to be asleep. As usual Kate peeked in each room to see if the girls were all right. Amanda thought her mother was crying.

The house was dark and quiet when Amanda heard her door open. She sat up in bed. "Who's there?"

"It's me. I'm scared. Can I come into your bed for a while?"

"All right." Amanda moved over to make room. "What scared you?" she asked as Lisa climbed in beside her.

"I don't know. I'm just scared."

"Were you thinking about Walter?"

"I guess so."

"I think Daddy's mean not to let you go."

"Maybe he'll change his mind." Lisa sighed. "Walter was so nice."

"Go to sleep now." Amanda turned on her side.

After a few minutes Lisa said, "Do you think Mommy and Daddy love each other?"

"I don't know. They fight a lot."

"Do you think they're going to get divorced?" Lisa's voice was small and frightened.

"I don't think so," Amanda said, hoping she sounded more convincing than she felt. "Go to sleep now. Think about something nice."

"I'll try," Lisa said.

Lisa's question stayed in the back of Amanda's mind all the next day at school. On her way home she decided to stop in to see her grandmother. She had no clear intention of talking about it, but after she had made her grandmother and herself some ginger tea and helped herself generously to cookies, the question popped out.

"Do you think my mother and my father love each other?"

"What a question! I imagine they do. Why do you ask?"

"They're always quarreling."

"People quarrel when they live together. It can't be helped. It doesn't mean they don't love each other."

"Did you quarrel with Grandpa when he was alive?"

"Sometimes. Of course."

"Do you quarrel with Mr. Adams?"

Margo laughed. "I don't live with Michael. But sometimes we quarrel anyway."

"Grandma, what does it feel like to be in love? I mean how do you know?"

"Gee whiz, that's a hard question. Poets have been trying to describe it for centuries. I guess it's when you want to be with someone all the time. When you feel lonely and adrift without the other person. When you want to share everything with him—your thoughts, your feelings, your experiences."

"Do you feel that way about Mr. Adams?"

"Hey, what is this? Michael Adams and I are good friends, that's all."

"Mommy thinks you're going to marry him."

"Does she?"

"I hope you don't get married," Amanda said.

"Why not?" Her grandmother looked surprised.

"Wouldn't you go live in his house?"

"I don't know. I rather think he'd come here. I wouldn't want to give up my house."

"It would be different though. I couldn't just come to see you whenever I wanted."

"Why not? Of course you could. Michael likes you and Lisa very much. Sometimes I tease him that he wants to marry me for my grandchildren, since he has none of his own. It wouldn't be any different."

"Oh, it would," Amanda insisted. "He'd probably like Lisa best anyway, the way Daddy does. Men don't like me very much, boys either. I don't suppose I'll ever get married. I don't really care, marriage is pretty dumb I think."

"Some marriages are good and some aren't. That goes for any relationship, Amanda. It depends on how much you want to make it work. Sisters, parents and kids." Her grandmother put down her teacup. "You know what I'm talking about."

"My father and me?"

"Right. Parents have feelings too, you know, the same as kids. A grown man like your father can get hurt just the same as you when you reject him. We hear an awful lot about children being rejected by their parents, but it can work the other way too. Everyone needs affection."

"He doesn't give me a chance." Amanda started to chew her nail nervously.

"Maybe he feels the same way." Her grandmother sighed. "It's hard. Michael says I'm too independent, but I like my editing work, and I don't want to give it up. Michael wants to cut down on his work and travel more. If we ever do get married it means a compromise for both of us. That's what getting along is all about."

Amanda still felt uneasy when she left her grandmother's. On the way home Randy Smyrski passed her on the street. He waved hello and kept walking, but on the corner he stopped to talk to two girls from school. Drat Randy Smyrski.

When Amanda got home Lisa called her into her room. "Will you help me write a letter to Walter telling him I can't go to see him in New York? I don't know how to say it."

"Aren't you going to go?"

"You heard Daddy. He won't let me."

"Why don't you go anyway?"

Lisa stared at her sister. "How could I? I'd be too scared."

"I'd go. Honestly, you make me sick the way you never stand up to Daddy. Don't you ever get mad at him? He's a pain in the neck."

Lisa stared at her sister helplessly. "Not really. I guess I'm not like you. I'm glad Walter asked me, but I'd be nervous going down to the city alone. Anyway, getting mad isn't going to change Daddy's mind."

Amanda shook her head, partly in amazement, partly in grudging admiration. "You know, I think you're smarter than I am. I can't even help getting angry, I just do." She sighed. "Come on, let's write your letter. Maybe he'll write you back," she added with a grin of sympathy.

Chapter Four

❖❖❖❖❖❖❖❖❖❖❖❖❖❖❖❖❖❖❖❖❖❖❖❖❖❖❖❖❖❖❖❖❖❖❖

FEBRUARY ENDED BUT THE WEATHER STAYED WET AND cold. One chilly Friday afternoon in early March Lisa felt bored and out of sorts. Her best friend Fran was at home with a sore throat and she had nothing to do. "You want to play a game?" She stuck her head in Amanda's room.

"Can't you see I'm busy?" Amanda sat at her desk writing in her journal.

"You're always writing in that journal. What do you put in it anyway?"

"None of your business. Very private thoughts. You wouldn't even understand them."

"How do you know? I bet I would. Try me, you'll see."

Amanda turned around in her chair. "Listen, if you ever dare to look in my journal, you'll be dead. I mean it."

"Who cares about your old journal anyway?" Lisa wandered back to her own room feeling glum. Amanda was really impossible. One day she was friendly and the next day she was just plain mean.

Lisa picked up a book but she didn't really feel like reading. When she heard her mother come in, she ran downstairs. Her mother greeted her with a hug and a kiss and headed upstairs. **2109406**

"Hi, Amanda," she called and went into her own room.

"You want to play a game?" Lisa asked, tagging behind.

"Not now," her mother said. "I'm tired. I think I'll stretch out for a while before it's time to start dinner."

Lisa drifted back to her own room. A moment later she heard Amanda go into her parents' room. Her mother couldn't be sleeping if Amanda was in there talking to her. She decided to go in too, but Amanda stopped her at the door. "I'm having a private conversation with Mommy," she said. "Please don't come in."

"Mommy said she wanted to rest. How come you can go in there and I can't?" How could they be so unfair?

"I do want to rest," Kate said from her bed. "But Amanda had something important she wanted to talk about. I'll play a game with you later if there's time before supper."

"There won't be. I know you."

"Don't be so pessimistic."

Lisa went back to her room and stared out the window, feeling angry and cut off. For a moment she wished that her father were home, so he could play a game with her. But she knew she really didn't care about playing: what she wanted more than anything was to know what Amanda and her mother were talking about. It was so mean, she thought, for people in a family to have secrets from one another.

Amanda's face was troubled as she sat at the foot of her mother's bed. "He didn't tell me, his friend Spitz did." She explained that Randy Smyrski had sent a message to her via Spitz. The message was that Randy liked her but thought she was stuck-up. The important part of the message was that he hoped she was coming to the school dance on Saturday night.

"If he wants you to come to the dance why doesn't he take you?"

Amanda gave her head a shake. "We don't do that. Nobody does. I usually go with Barbara and we just meet everyone there."

"So what's the problem? Go with Barbara and you'll meet him there."

"But Barbara doesn't want to go. None of my friends want to go. They say only older kids will be there."

"How old is Randy?"

"I don't know. Fourteen, I guess. Maybe almost fifteen."

"For heaven's sake, that's not so much older. If you want to go, go by yourself. Some day you'll have to learn to go alone."

"Oh, I couldn't do that," Amanda said. "I'd be scared to." Then she asked, "Do you think I'm stuck-up?"

"No, I don't. But Randy might if you never talk to him. Why don't you?"

"I feel shy. He makes me feel funny, different from the way I feel about other boys."

"So what are you going to do?"

"I don't know. What should I do?"

"If I were you I'd try to persuade Barbara to go to the dance with you. Even if she did it as a favor. That's what friends are for. When you get there I think things will take care of themselves with Randy."

"But what if it's awful? What if Barbara and I don't like it—I mean if there are only older kids there?"

"You can always call up and Dad or I will come and get you. Don't worry about that."

Amanda kissed her mother with relief and went downstairs to call Barbara.

A moment later Lisa heard her mother call, "Lisa, come in and talk to me."

She ran in promptly and sat down on her mother's bed. "What should we talk about?"

"I don't care, anything you want."

"What did you and Amanda talk about?"

"A private problem of Amanda's. Let's talk about you. How are things at school?"

"Okay." Suddenly Lisa felt confused, at a loss for something to say. She got up and walked aimlessly around the room. "Are you sorry you have two daughters?" she asked abruptly.

"Of course not! What on earth made you ask that?"

"I don't know." Then Lisa laughed.

"What's funny?"

"I was thinking of Miss Evans," Lisa said, "the French teacher. The boys laugh at her because she sticks way out in front. They call her Miss Boobs."

"That's not very nice," said her mother. "I hope you don't laugh at her, sweetie."

"Sometimes I do." Lisa studied her profile in the mirror and wondered what to say next. "Do you think I'll ever get big in front?" she asked finally.

"You'll get bigger than you are, but I don't think you'll get very big. Come over here."

Obediently Lisa sat down on the bed. Her mother gave her a hug. "I'm very glad you're my daughter, don't ever forget that."

"I'm glad too," Lisa said, nuzzling up against her. Then she got up again. "Are you as glad about me as you are about Amanda?"

"Of course I am. You know that. I love you both the same. The way you love Daddy and me the same, I hope."

"Yeah, sure." But Lisa wasn't convinced. She felt let down. Their talk should have been more interesting, more serious. Amanda and her mother always looked as if they were confiding important things to one another, things that mattered—not just stuff like Miss Evans and bust development. Lisa headed downstairs to the kitchen. Maybe a sandwich would make her feel better.

Saturday Amanda was nervous. She had persuaded Barbara to go to the dance with her, and the two girls met downtown in the afternoon. "Why did he ask Spitz to say that to me?" Amanda wondered aloud.

"I guess he wanted you to know he liked you but he was too shy to talk to you himself."

"But it makes me feel funny. I want him to know I'm not stuck-up, but how do I do it? I can't go up to him and say, 'See, I'm not stuck-up.' Anyway, why does he think that about me?"

"Oh, you know," Barbara said. "He's a townie and you're not. His father works in a garage and your father's an architect. You know what I mean. They live over in that development your father called an eyesore in that letter he sent to the paper."

"That was a couple of years ago. Besides, Randy can't blame me for that. It wasn't my fault."

"I know, but he probably thinks you're stuck-up because of your father. I think you should talk to him tonight."

"Oh-h-h . . . I get nervous thinking about it."

When Amanda came home in the early evening she found her mother dressing to go out. "I thought you and Dad were staying home tonight."

"Oh, a client of Dad's invited us out for dinner and to the theater."

"Then how can I call you if I want to come home early?"

"I guess you can't. We'll pick you up a little after eleven. We'll come right from the playhouse."

Amanda's heart dropped. "But you promised! We may not want to stay there that long."

"Can't one of Barbara's parents get you then?"

"No, they're away. I said we'd take her home."

"Then you'll just have to stay. Don't worry, you'll have a good time. You'll probably beg to stay when we come for you."

"I don't know," Amanda said. She went to her room to look over her clothes. She had decided to wear a pink sweater and a navy skirt, but now she wasn't sure about the sweater. Maybe her light blue one would look better.

Lisa came into her room. "What programs do you want to watch tonight?"

"I'm not watching any. I'm going out."

"You can't go out. Mom and Dad are going out and I can't stay here alone."

"I'm going to a dance. Why don't you ask Fran to come over?"

"She went to her grandmother's." Lisa ran across the hall to her parents' room. The door was open and she walked in. Her mother was putting on her shoes and her father was adjusting his tie in front of the mirror.

"Amanda says she's going out and now you're going out. I'm not going to stay home alone." Lisa was close to tears.

"You can ask a friend over," her mother said.

"Fran went to her grandmother's and there's no one else. Make Amanda stay home."

"It wouldn't hurt her ... she could bone up on her math."

"Oh, Mark, you can't be serious!" Kate looked at her husband reproachfully. "She's going to a dance tonight. You have other friends beside Fran," she said to Lisa. "What about Joan? You can ask her over."

"She's away for the weekend. I've got no one," Lisa wailed. "I'm not staying home alone."

Kate turned a troubled face to Mark. "I suppose she's old enough to stay home by herself ..."

"No! I'm not staying home alone." Lisa turned a pleading face to her father. "Daddy, I don't have to, do I?"

"No, not if you don't feel comfortable about it."

"I don't. So what are you going to do?" Lisa looked from one parent to the other.

"I don't know," said Kate. "I am not going to ask Amanda to stay in. It just wouldn't be fair. I'd rather stay home myself. I don't even know the people we're going out with." She gave her husband a worried glance and looked in the mirror to adjust her hair. "You're babying Lisa again," she added in a murmur.

"Don't start in on that," Mark snapped. "If the kid doesn't want to stay home alone she shouldn't. I could say you want everyone to accommodate Amanda."

"That's right," Lisa said. She was sorry she had spoken when she saw the expression on her mother's face.

"Go ahead, then. Say it," said her mother coldly.

"Oh, for Christ's sake," said Mark. "I'll call my mother and ask her to come over."

Lisa walked out of the room, frightened. She hated it when her parents fought like that, especially when they fought about her and Amanda. It made her feel that neither one of them should ever have been born.

It was a relief when they left and she was alone in the house with her grandmother. For a while they watched television together and then Lisa made her way up to bed. She was just falling asleep when she heard a car door slam and realized that it was her parents. A moment later she heard her father's voice. It was angry.

"This time you stay out of it; I'll handle it. Amanda is simply not going to get away with this! Almost midnight and we don't know where the devil she is! That's what you get for being so soft with her."

"Let's find out what happened, before you read the riot act." Her mother's voice was level.

"I don't care what happened," her father yelled. "There's no excuse in the world for her not to be there when we're supposed to pick her up!"

"I don't suppose you do care what happened." There

was a pause. "I didn't mean that," she added. "Of course you care. We're both upset and worried . . . where can she be?"

"I wish I knew. Maybe we should call the police."

Suddenly the phone rang, and Lisa, who had been getting more and more frightened, came pattering down in her bathrobe. Her mother answered the phone; her face was white when she hung up. "She's at the police station. They asked us to come get her."

"Is she all right?" asked Margo.

"I guess so. The sergeant said no one was hurt. Come on," she said to Mark.

His face was tense as he made for the door. Lisa ran after him and tugged at his coat. "I'm scared," she said.

"For heaven's sake, Lisa, we're in a hurry," he answered impatiently.

"You stay here with Grandma," her mother bent to give her a quick kiss. "Everything will be all right, don't worry."

Lisa watched them go with a sinking heart, and climbed up into her grandmother's lap.

At best the local police station was not a homey-looking place, but that night Kate thought it the most forlorn room she had ever entered, with its bare walls and wooden benches. The sergeant sitting at the huge desk, however, did not look unfriendly. He and the young officer with him had been around the town for a number of years,

Kate knew. Amanda and Barbara were huddled together on one of the benches and both girls looked as if they had been crying. Randy Smyrski was standing with his father talking to the young officer.

Amanda ran to her mother's arms and buried her head against her shoulder. "We didn't do anything wrong . . . Randy was doing us a favor, it wasn't his fault, he was just going to take us home and bring the car right back . . ."

Mark gave her an awkward pat on the back. "At least you're in one piece, thank God." He turned to the sergeant. "What's the story?"

"Nothing that involves the girls, except they could have had more sense," the officer said. "We picked up young Smyrski here driving without a license, and a couple of six-packs of beer in the car, so we had to bring him in. The girls just need a ride home."

"What were you doing in a car with this boy?" Her father turned to Amanda.

"He was taking us home, that's all. No one even knew there was beer in the car. He wasn't doing anything wrong."

"He was driving without a license."

"But they had no reason to stop him," objected Mr. Smyrski. He was a big man with a genial, ruddy face. "He wasn't even disobeying a traffic law," he said. "Just doing the girls a favor because they wanted to go home."

"Listen, mister," said the younger officer, "when you see a kid who looks too young to be driving in a car with a couple of girls late at night, it's a smart thing to stop them to see what's going on. And I was right, wasn't I? Him driving a car and not yet fifteen."

"I'm not saying my son was right, he wasn't. But you weren't right either. You don't stop people for the way they look. You've got to have a good, legal reason to stop a car and ask to see a license. We're not yet living in a state where anyone can be stopped for an identification card."

"So, sue me." The young officer shrugged.

"I probably could if I wanted to. But I'm willing to forget it if you do. I don't want any police record against my son. He made a mistake and I guarantee you he'll never do it again, so let's call it quits." Mr. Smyrski looked up at the sergeant.

"I object to that," Mark cut in. "He should be punished. He had my daughter and her friend in the car—two innocent girls who might have been hurt or killed with an irresponsible kid driving. You can't let him get away with it."

"What do you want us to do, lock him up?" the sergeant asked mildly.

"What you do is your business. But I consider it wrong to let this boy go scot-free."

For the first time Mr. Smyrski turned to Mark. "It just happens that my son drives a car better than most of my customers, but that's neither here nor there. The point is, your daughter was *not* hurt, nobody was hurt, and if this cop was minding his own business, we all of us would be home in bed right now. Cops go out of their way to get kids and I don't like it. In the meantime the muggers and robbers are doing their dirty work while this guy here is fooling around with nonsense." He turned to the sergeant. "Is it a deal, officer?"

The sergeant nodded. "Okay. I won't put anything on the books. But if we ever catch him driving before he gets his license, he'll be in real trouble."

"You hear that, Randy?" asked his father.

"Yes, sir." Randy had been silent while the men were talking. Now he turned to Mr. Dobson. "I'm sorry I caused all this trouble. I only meant to help the girls. It won't happen again."

"You're darn right it won't happen again. Whether you have a license or not I promise you my daughter won't be driving around with Randy Smyrski!"

"A name that is better than most," Mr. Smyrski said angrily. "Come on, Randy, let's go." He strode out of the police station with Randy at his heels.

With a grim face Mark herded his wife and the two girls into his car. No one spoke until after Barbara had been dropped off at her house.

"You didn't have to be so mean to Randy," Amanda said timidly. "He didn't mean to do anything wrong."

"I don't want to talk about it any more tonight. We'll discuss it in the morning," Mark said.

"Why do you have to make up the rules of what to talk about and when?" Kate muttered.

"What did you say?" Mark asked.

She repeated it in a louder voice. "Go on, turn Amanda against me again, like you always do." Mark slammed on the brakes for a red light.

"I didn't notice you sticking up for her. It was beautiful the way Mr. Smyrski stuck up for his son," Kate said.

"That's right," said Amanda, suddenly envious of Randy.

"You be quiet," her father said. "I don't want to hear anything from you tonight."

About half an hour later Amanda lay in bed listening to her parents in their room. They were fighting again.

"It's kids like Randy who grow up to be bums," her father was saying. "You let them get away with a few things and the next thing you know they're mugging old ladies."

"You're absolutely wrong," his wife retorted. "It's because his father trusts and respects him that he'll never *be* a bum. That boy had a lesson tonight he'll never forget, and probably the most important part was having his father's trust. He won't betray that in a hurry."

"What are you trying to tell me? That I don't trust Amanda? Well, you're right. She used lousy judgment getting into a car with that boy, and I'd be a lousy father if I didn't let her know it."

"There are other ways of doing it," said Kate. "You only want to be a father when it comes to correcting and criticizing. The rest of the time you're no father to Amanda at all. You show up when it's time to punish or discipline—you've got no other relationship with her, only with Lisa."

"You seem to be harping on that a lot lately. What's the matter, jealous of your own daughter?"

"Oh, my God, you would think of that. No, I'm not jealous of my daughter, but I think you need reminding that you have two daughters, not one."

"Well, I can say the same to you. Half the time you don't know Lisa exists, you're so busy defending Amanda or whispering with her about something. You're on pretty shaky ground there, I'm afraid."

"The same old tactic. Attacking me to defend yourself. Well, if you don't mind, I'm going to sleep."

"I don't mind. I'll read downstairs."

Amanda saw the light go out in their room and heard her father going down the stairs. She lay in her bed blinking back the tears. It was all her fault—their fights, their bitter quarrels. If she hadn't been born they'd probably be very happy. She thought of her father sitting downstairs by himself, and suddenly she felt terribly sorry for him. He always got such a strained, bewildered look on his face when they had those quarrels. She wondered if her mother really did love him—she tried to remember when she'd last seen her mother go and put her arms around him or laugh at his jokes the way she used to. Amanda was tempted to go downstairs to tell her father that she loved him and that she knew he wanted to be a good father, but she was afraid she'd sound foolish or maybe cry.

Chapter Five

❖❖❖❖❖❖❖❖❖❖❖❖❖❖❖❖❖❖❖❖❖❖❖❖❖❖❖❖❖❖❖❖❖❖

SUNDAY MORNING AMANDA SAT WAITING WITH A HEAVY heart for her father to finish reading the *New York Times.* He had said he wanted to talk to her after he'd looked at the paper. So far he hadn't even finished the News section and she wondered if he was going to read all the other sections as thoroughly. She let out a big sigh when he picked up the bulky *Book Review.* "Are you going to read all that before you talk to me?"

"Sure," her father said cheerfully from his big leather chair. "And the Sports section, and Real Estate and

Travel and Finance." He looked down at her with a grin. "Every word."

"Oh, Daddy . . ." Amanda was woebegone.

He laughed and put down the newspaper. "Okay. What do you think? Don't you think you should get some punishment for last night?"

"I suppose so. Although I don't think I did anything so awful."

"No, it wasn't so awful, but something pretty awful could have happened. Cars are dangerous and you need to learn right now that you can't get into a car with just anyone."

"Randy's not anyone."

"Let's not talk about Randy. Well, let's see. Today's half gone, so supposing you stay in the rest of today and next Saturday night. That's not too bad, is it?"

"It's terrible. Barbara and I were going to go for a hike this afternoon."

"I guess you can't. It looks as if it might rain anyway. She could come over here."

"I don't want to stay in. And next Saturday night too! That's too much. Can't it just be today?"

"I think not. I said the rest of today and Saturday night. Now I really do want to read the paper."

"That's mean. You were mean last night to Randy and now you're mean to me." Amanda stood up.

Mark put down the paper. "Take it easy, Amanda. You gave us a lot of worry and trouble last night and I've been trying to be fair with you. It wasn't any fun not knowing where you were and then getting a call from the police station." He pointed a finger at her. "I'm warning you, don't push me."

"You're not fair, you're never fair with me. God, I wish I didn't have to live in this house. You just say stay home, you don't even know or care what I'd planned to do. Next Saturday night could be the most important night of my life and you'd still make me stay home. I don't call that fair!"

"I doubt that next Saturday night will be the most important night of your life." Mark looked at her with a grin. "You weren't planning to get married, were you?"

"It's not funny," Amanda yelled. "You're . . . you're . . . you're sadistic." She finally found the right word. "You love torture!"

Mark got to his feet, visibly angry. "I'm not going to keep my temper forever. I think you'd better go up to your room and stay there until you can behave rationally."

Amanda ran up to her room, slammed her door shut and flung herself on her bed. She lay there wishing she'd saved her Christmas money instead of spending it all on records and clothes. If she had it now she could run away, but she knew she couldn't get far on a dollar and eighty-three cents, and that was all she had left.

And how could she get a message to Barbara to tell her she wasn't coming over? She absolutely would not go out of her room to use the phone! She would stay inside until it was time to go to school on Monday morning, and even then she wasn't sure she'd leave. Maybe, she thought, she would just stay in her room forever. She'd die of starvation. Then her father would be sorry for the way he'd treated her.

Minutes later Lisa burst in. "You have to stay in your room all day?"

"Haven't I told you to knock before you come bombing in here? Now will you please get out and stay out?"

Lisa stood in the doorway. "I'm sorry, Amanda. You want me to bring you something to eat?"

Amanda softened. "Maybe later. I'm not hungry now. But don't let Daddy see you." Then she sat up with an idea. "Listen, can you do me a favor?"

"Sure." Lisa's eyes sparkled.

"Will you go over to Barbara's and tell her I can't come over? Tell her I'll see her in school tomorrow. But, Lisa, don't let Daddy know where you're going."

"Doesn't he want you to see Barbara anymore?" Lisa's eyes widened with surprise.

"No, it's just . . . well, I just don't want him to know anything about me."

"Are you going to have a secret life?" Lisa asked with delight.

"I'm not going to have any life," Amanda said glumly.

"Daddy'll get over it. He'll forget all about it by supper time."

"Not with me he won't. Besides, I won't forget. I'll never forget how mean he is."

"He's only mean once in a while."

"Not to me he isn't. Get going, will you?"

Amanda dug her journal out of her bureau drawer and held it across her knees. For a while she just held it, wondering how she could ever express the confusion of thoughts and feelings that was piling up inside her. Then she began to write:

I am not going to let my father ruin my life. When I am sixteen I intend to leave home and no one can stop me. I think it will be legal then, I'm not sure. I don't care if it isn't, I'll do it anyway. I think Randy Smyrski likes me, and I think he knows I am not stuck-up. I hope he won't be mad at me because of my father. My father is the one who is stuck-up. Because he's smart and knows a lot he thinks he's better than anyone else. I bet Mr. Smyrski's just as smart as he is even if he never went to college. Maybe he did, how should I know? Anyway I don't think it matters what kind of a house people live in. A person who works in a garage can't help getting greasy and he's just as good as an architect. My father gets dirty when he works on his car too. My father thinks he has a right to boss me around, but I don't think anyone should boss another person even if he is older and your father. If I ever have children (probably not because I don't intend to get married) I will never boss them.

By the time Lisa came back and reported that Barbara was going out with her parents and was sorry Amanda was stuck inside, Amanda was feeling better. "What's for dinner?" she asked.

"I don't know," Lisa said. "Should I bring some up?"

"Find out what it is first."

Lisa ran downstairs and came back quickly to report. "Roast beef, roast potatoes, carrots and salad. Leftover cake for dessert."

"After dinner, when everyone's finished, bring me up a roast-beef sandwich. Try not to let anyone see you. Slice the bread thin and use lots of mustard. A glass of milk, too, if you can carry it."

"Okay." Lisa grinned. "This is fun. It's like you were a hideaway. Maybe you should go live in the attic."

Amanda pondered the idea for a second. "It would get boring."

Lisa continued to look at her older sister. "Am I your friend now?"

Amanda frowned. "That's a silly question. We're sisters. We'll always be sisters."

"I know that. But can't we be friends too?"

"I don't know. It's hard for people in the same family to be friends."

"I don't see why. Mommy and Daddy are friends, aren't they?"

"No, they're not friends. They're husband and wife. If they were friends they wouldn't fight so much."

"I wish they didn't, don't you? I wonder why they do."

"Because of us," said Amanda with conviction. "If they didn't have kids I bet they wouldn't fight."

"If they didn't have kids they wouldn't be married," retorted Lisa.

Something about this statement struck Amanda, and she wondered if her parents were together only because they had two daughters. Somehow the thought was like an unsolved puzzle.

Just then they heard their mother call Lisa to come downstairs.

"Come and help me set the table," said Kate. She ran her hand over the smooth, gleaming wood of the dining room table. "I love this," she said. "It was the first thing Dad and I bought after we got married. We didn't have any furniture, or any money—we were sleeping on a mattress on the floor! Then I saw this in an antique store and fell in love with it. It was much too expensive for us to buy then, but when your father got his first big design job several months later, he went back and got it."

"That was nice of him, wasn't it?"

"Very nice." Kate handed Lisa the silverware.

"Do you like Daddy?"

"Of course I do. What a question!"

"You don't always act like you do."

Kate stopped putting out napkins and faced Lisa. "Daddy and I don't always agree about everything. But that doesn't mean we don't care for each other."

Lisa didn't answer. "Call Amanda for dinner," her mother said.

"She's not coming down. She's staying in her room all day."

Kate frowned. "I wish ..." but she didn't finish her

sentence. "I guess we'd better eat. I'll go up and see Amanda later. Maybe if she's alone for a while she'll cool off."

Lisa and her parents had just sat down to eat when the phone rang. Kate ran to answer it and came back in a few minutes looking unhappy.

"I've got to go to the office. Some clients have just shown up wanting to see the Barker house."

Mark continued carving silently, and handed Kate a plate of food.

"I'll just fix a quick sandwich and run."

"They can wait till after dinner."

"These people have come from quite a distance. I don't want to keep them waiting."

"Damn it, can't this family even have a Sunday dinner together?" Mark slammed his hand down on the table.

"You're the one who sent Amanda to her room," said Kate as she slapped some meat between two slices of bread.

"Only for a while because she was fresh. Now she's up there sulking."

"Well, I'll see you later." Kate picked up her sandwich, gave Lisa a kiss and left.

Lisa loved roast beef and her father had given her her favorite, the crisp end piece, but now she found she wasn't hungry.

"I guess it's just the two of us again," her father said morosely. "At least we have each other," he added with an attempt at a smile.

"Gives us more to eat," Lisa said, wanting to cheer him up. He looked so unhappy. "It's nice to be with you, Daddy."

"And it's nice to be with you."

But they ate most of their meal in silence. The fun had gone out of the day for Lisa. Even the thought of sneaking a sandwich up to Amanda wasn't exciting anymore. It would have been really nice to have dinner with her parents without Amanda, but being alone with her father wasn't the same. She felt abandoned.

Her father cut into her thoughts. "I don't know why your mother couldn't have finished her dinner. Damn it, I hate her running off like this. No client is that important. Her family should come first."

"You go off when you have to go to work," Lisa said. "Mom can do it too."

Her father gave her an appraising look. "You don't look very happy about it, though. I thought you said it was nice being here alone with me."

"Sometimes it is."

"But not always?"

Lisa shook her head impatiently. "I don't want to talk about it."

Her father ate his food in silence for a few minutes. "For God's sake, what's going on in this house? Everyone's so jumpy." He put down his fork. "Come on, baby, give us a smile."

"Why don't you leave me alone? I don't feel like smiling and I'm not your baby." Lisa pushed away her plate. "I don't feel like eating anymore. Can I be excused?"

"No, you cannot. Not until you tell me what's bugging you. First your sister, then your mother, now you. It's too much."

"Maybe it's you. Did you ever think of that?"

"Yes, I think about it a lot." Mark's face was serious. "But what did I do now? You tell me."

Lisa stared at her father for a few seconds and then turned away. "I can't," she mumbled. She couldn't tell her father that sometimes she wished he didn't fuss over her so much, as if she was a baby. If he left her alone and didn't treat her like his special pet, she'd get on better with her mother and her sister, and she wouldn't feel so left out. Lisa wished she could explain, but it was too complicated.

"Well, don't look so unhappy. You've always got me," he said, giving her a pat.

"Yeah, I know," Lisa said dolefully.

Mark laughed. "That's telling me. I'm not enough, am I?"

No, she thought. I want a mother *and* a father. She gave him a weak smile, and gathered up their dishes to take into the kitchen. She was making a sandwich for Amanda when her father came in.

"For your sister?" he asked. To her nod he said, "You're a good kid, Lisa. While you're at it, give her a piece of cake."

Her face brightened. "That's a good idea. You're okay too."

"Amanda doesn't think so," he sighed.

Chapter Six

❖◆❖◆❖◆❖◆❖◆❖◆❖◆❖◆❖◆❖◆❖◆❖◆❖◆❖◆❖◆❖◆❖◆❖◆❖◆❖

ALL WEEK LONG AMANDA TRIED TO FIGURE OUT HOW SHE
could get out on Saturday night. "Can't you tell him
you'll stay in all day Sunday again? Just to switch it?"
Barbara asked. She and Amanda were sprawled on the
floor of her room, with the stereo going. Amanda thought
Barbara's room was a little crazy, but she liked it. Barbara
had started to do the room over, but so far had only gotten the old wallpaper ripped off. She had taped some rock
posters to one wall and had tacked up an old fur coat of
her mother's, cut up to make a hanging, on the other.
There was a fish tank on her desk and a chipmunk in a

cage who turned somersaults all day long. He never seemed to get tired but Barbara swore to Amanda that he slept at night.

"He picked out Saturday night because he knows that's the worst. My father can really be mean," said Amanda.

"I suppose I'm lucky. My father just gave me a lecture. Said I had no business driving with a kid, and a lot of other stuff, but that was all."

"You are lucky," Amanda agreed. She got up to change the record.

Barbara looked up at Amanda. "I don't think they care much about me anyway. I can do pretty much what I like."

"Be glad you don't have someone picking on you all the time like I do."

"Yeah." Barbara nodded but she didn't sound convinced.

By the time Saturday came around Amanda had gotten nowhere. It was St. Patrick's Day and her friends had been planning a party at Barbara's house all week. Amanda had felt completely left out while they talked about it.

"It isn't fair," she complained to her mother in the kitchen that morning. "I'm going to have to be home all alone." Lisa was going to sing in a play at school and her parents were going to see her.

"I wish Daddy would let you come with us. It wouldn't really be like going out."

"I don't care if I don't go to the play."

"That's good, because you're not going anywhere," her father said, as he walked into the kitchen.

"I do think she could come to school," Kate said.

"There you go, undermining me."

"Nuts! If I disagree with you it's 'undermining.' If you disagree with me 'everyone has a right to a different opinion.' Why don't you use the same language for both of us?"

Amanda wished she could close her ears. She couldn't stand to listen to them have another argument. "Forget it," she said. "I may as well be living in a police state. I'll lose my friends, I won't have any fun until I get out of here for good. But—" she turned to her father—"if you think I'm going to work on my math you're wrong. I don't care if I flunk it. I hope I do."

"If you think you're threatening me," Mark said with a half smile, "you are wrong. And stop feeling so sorry for yourself. As a matter of fact you're getting off pretty easy for what you did. You're lucky you weren't killed."

"I wish I had been," Amanda said. "Anything would be better than living in this prison."

"Amanda, don't say things like that," her mother implored. "It's just one night. Tomorrow it'll be all over."

"I may be dead by tomorrow. This is my only chance to go to a St. Patrick's Day party. I've never been to one, and I'll probably never get invited to one again."

"On the other hand you may be going to St. Patrick's

Day parties for years to come." Her father laughed. "Everything is so dramatic and final with you. Staying home for one night is not the end of the world."

"I hate you," Amanda yelled, and ran out of the room. He had laughed at her! If she were a man, she would have hit him, he made her so angry. He didn't have to stay in on Saturday night. He didn't have to worry that Randy Smyrski would think she was a real baby because her parents kept her home from the party. Her father was hopeless. For all his college education and the graduate work he was so proud of he didn't know anything about girls or how people felt or how to be a father. Mr. Smyrski in his garage knew more about being a father than Mr. Mark Dobson did!

Thinking about Mr. Smyrski made her think about Randy all over again. She happened to know that he was going to the party tonight because of her. And she didn't have the heart to tell him that she wouldn't be there. Besides, until now she had hoped that her father might change his mind. No matter what, she couldn't tell Randy that she was being kept in like a ten-year-old because she'd ridden in the car with him. Amanda sat in her room brooding.

Lisa spent the afternoon waiting for the evening. She had never been in a play before, and since she intended to be a musical star she felt this first opportunity was important. The play was a fairy tale and Lisa was the good fairy. She had wanted to be the princess who married the prince in the end, but another girl got that part. However, she was comforted by the knowledge that she had a beautiful long, white, silky costume to wear and that her face was going to be made up with eyeshadow, lipstick, rouge and a little black beauty mark.

Lisa alternated between being eager for the evening to come and dreading it nervously. She ran into Amanda's room a few times just to talk to someone, but after her third visit Amanda yelled at her. "Can't you see I want to be left alone? Stop bothering me."

"You could at least try to be interested in your own sister's first play. I'll be a famous star some day and you'll be sorry."

"I won't be sorry at all. I'll be glad if you go live in Hollywood or wherever stars live. I wish you luck."

"I'm glad you have to stay home tonight because you're so mean."

"You would be glad. You get everything you want and you don't care about anyone else."

"That's not true. I care about my cat," Lisa said, picking up her cat from Amanda's bed and flouncing out. Amanda laughed. Lisa looked silly dressed only in her slip, wearing her gold fairy queen crown and holding the big, squirming cat.

But she didn't laugh for long. Everyone in the house was getting ready for the evening, and the thought of staying home alone made Amanda feel stifled, claustrophobic. Suddenly she couldn't bear to stay in her room another minute. She grabbed a sweater and went down-stairs.

"Where are you going?" her father called out as she headed for the door.

"Just over to Grandma's."

"If you think she's going to get me to change my mind you're wrong."

"I hadn't even thought of that," Amanda said indignantly. "You're too mean to change your mind anyway."

"Sure, I'm the big bad wolf," he said mockingly.

Amanda walked into the village to her grandmother's 1790 house on Main Street. Margo was in the kitchen pressing a long black dress.

After greeting her grandmother with a kiss, Amanda sat down at the kitchen table. "I suppose you're going out to-night too."

"Yes, I am. What's making you so glum?"

Amanda told her grandmother that she had to stay in that evening. "Daddy doesn't have to be so mean. My friend Barbara wasn't punished at all, and neither was Randy. It isn't as if we hurt anyone."

"Maybe your father is upset because he really cares about you. You might have been hurt with such a young kid driving."

"Maybe ... but we weren't hurt." She changed the subject.

"You going out with Mr. Adams?"

"Yes."

"Are you going to get married?"

"You've asked me that before. We may. Wouldn't you like to go to a wedding?"

Amanda's eyes lit up. "Would you be dressed like a bride, all in white, with a long veil?"

Margo laughed. "Good heavens, no. I'm too old for that. I'd just wear something simple."

"I don't see why. I think you should look like a bride." Amanda's mind turned back to her own troubles. "If Daddy would only let me go to Barbara's party tonight, I could stay in next Saturday night."

"I think you're better off getting it over with. You wouldn't like staying in any more next Saturday than tonight."

"But tonight is special."

"I'm sure next Saturday will be too."

"He wouldn't do it anyway," Amanda said gloomily.

When she left her grandmother she walked home very slowly. If only she could keep on walking and not go home, she thought—find a place to hide where no one could find her.

"We won't be home late," Amanda's mother said before they left.

"You don't have to come home early for me. I don't care."

"Come on, hurry up, Mom," Lisa called from downstairs.

"I'm coming. . . . cheer up, honey, it's only one night." She kissed Amanda and left.

The front door closed behind them, and the house grew ominously silent. Feeling totally inert, Amanda lay on her bed and stared at the ceiling. A small black fly walked across it and she wondered if the fly was going to meet a friend to go out with on Saturday night. Maybe the two of them would go flying around together.

Amanda was roused out of her lethargy by the ringing of the phone. It was Barbara. "Have they all gone?" she asked.

"Yeah. I'm all alone."

"Why don't you come over?"

"You know I can't."

"They won't know the difference. Come over for a little while. School plays never start on time—it probably won't start till after eight. They can't possibly get home before ten, at the earliest. And I'm not that far from your house."

Amanda's heart had been thumping rapidly while she listened to Barbara. "You mean sneak out? I'm scared to."

"There's nothing to be scared of. Your father will never know. Come on. Randy's going to be here any minute. He'll be mad if you're not here. Don't you want to see him?"

"Sure I do. But . . ."

"Come on, hurry up. You're just wasting time on the phone. I'll expect you." Barbara hung up.

Amanda sat up on her bed for a moment. Then she jumped up and brushed her hair frantically. She got out of her jeans and shirt and put on a skirt and a blouse, and brushed her hair again. Ten minutes later she was ringing Barbara's bell.

When Barbara opened the door, Amanda rushed inside. "You took so long to open the door," she panted.

Barbara laughed. "No one is chasing you. Relax."

"Don't be crazy, I can't relax. I'm scared stiff. What if my father finds out?"

"He won't. He can't. You'll be home before he gets there," Barbara said reassuringly.

Randy came in a few minutes later with some of the other kids. When he came over and said hello to Amanda she felt shy and wondered why she'd been so anxious to see him. Maybe she was just too nervous to enjoy anything. Barbara put some records on and everyone sat around and talked. A few couples started dancing. After a short while Randy sat down on the floor beside her. Even though they didn't talk much his closeness felt good to Amanda, and she realized she was glad she had taken the risk to come.

Later, as she had promised, Barbara let her know it was a quarter to ten, and Amanda got up to leave.

"I'll walk you home," Randy said, and left with her.

Out on the street Amanda walked so fast she was almost running. "What's your hurry?" asked Randy.

"I'm not supposed to be out. I've got to get home before my parents."

"You mean you sneaked out?"

Amanda gave him a swift look. "Yes, I did."

He looked surprised. "Why'd you do it?"

"I don't know," she said, almost under her breath.

"Anything to do with me?"

Amanda kept up her pace. "In a way. I had to stay in because of what happened last Saturday. The car."

"I'm sorry you got into so much trouble."

"That's all right." She stopped for a second. "I'm glad I came out tonight."

"So am I," he said, meeting her eyes with a clear, level glance. They smiled at each other.

Amanda saw they were at her corner. "Goodbye," she called, and made a dash for her door.

She was on her bed, still out of breath, when she heard her father's car pull into the driveway. Quickly she ripped off her skirt and blouse and put on a bathrobe. She was quite composed when her parents and Lisa came into the house.

Lisa came running up the stairs and poked her head into Amanda's room. Then she called out, "She's here, Daddy. I told you she would be."

Amanda's heart started pounding. "What do you mean? Of course I'm here. Where would I be?"

Lisa came into the room. "Daddy was mad. He called up and there was no answer. He said you'd gone out."

"I was probably in the bathroom," Amanda said casually, but her heart was still thumping. She could hear her father coming up the stairs.

"I want to talk to Amanda, Lisa," he said as he came

into the room. He closed the door behind her, and sat down in the armchair.

"Where did you go, Amanda?" he asked, his face stern.

"I didn't go anywhere."

"Don't lie to me. I called here a few times. You were not home."

"Why'd you check up on me? You don't trust me, do you?"

"I have good reason not to, don't I? I know you better than you think. Now where were you?"

Amanda looked down at the quilt on her bed, and studied its design. She kept silent.

"Come on, speak up. Let's get this over with." Her father's face broke into troubled lines.

"I went over to Barbara's for a little while. I didn't think it was fair of you to keep me in."

"You didn't think it was fair! Damn it, Amanda, what do you know about fairness? Do you think it's fair to worry your parents sick? Do you think it's fair that I can't trust you? You're thirteen years old, you're not a baby anymore." He got up and began pacing the room. "I just don't know what to say. I can't believe that you would deliberately disobey me like this. It makes me sick, really sick. Don't you know what it means to keep your word?" He stopped and faced her. "Answer me," he yelled.

"I didn't promise anything," Amanda said defiantly. "I didn't hurt anyone. I'm a person, not a thing you can order around. You keep telling me I have bad judgment.

How am I ever going to learn anything if you never let me make any decisions? It's always, 'I want you to do this, I want you to do that.' Why can't *I* ever decide what to do?" She was close to tears.

Her mother walked into the room. "They can hear you two screaming all the way to the village. Do you have to yell so loud?" she asked her husband.

"Yes, I do, and even then this daughter of yours doesn't hear me."

"That's the trouble. You think she's my daughter and not yours. Perhaps if you were more of a father we wouldn't have all this yelling." She was as upset as he was.

"I don't want to be anybody's daughter," Amanda yelled. "I'm me, myself. Yes, I disobeyed you, and I'm glad I did. I'd do it all over again. You say you do things because you care about me, but it's not true. You hate me, and I'm never going to obey you. You're not God. You're a mean, lousy father," Amanda ended up, facing him with tears streaming down her face.

"Don't you talk to me that way, don't you dare." His voice shook. There was a resounding smack as his hand slapped Amanda's face.

Amanda threw herself across her bed, sobbing loudly. "Get out of here," she yelled. "Just get out."

The door slammed behind him. Her mother bent over Amanda. "Are you all right? Let me see your face. Did he hurt you?"

"Yes, he hurt me," Amanda sobbed. "Just leave me alone. I want to be alone."

"But I'm on your side. You may need some ice on your cheek. Let me see it."

"I don't need anything. I'll be all right, I just want to be by myself."

Her mother let out a sigh and left the room.

Amanda lay on her bed for a long while after she had cried herself out. She didn't know why she had turned away from her mother, except that the words "I'm on your side" had upset her. She didn't want sides, and she didn't want her mother's protection. She hated her father's picking on her, punishing her, but much as she loved her mother, the way her mother always intervened for her made her feel uncomfortable, like a baby who couldn't stand up for herself. Sometimes she almost wished that her mother would side with her father. Shouldn't parents stick together?

After Amanda got undressed and ready for bed she decided she was hungry. She crept downstairs softly in her bare feet, past her parents' closed door, and headed for the kitchen. She jumped in surprise when she passed by the living room: there was a figure stretched out on the sofa underneath a blanket. Her mother's head popped up. "Is that you, Amanda?"

"What are you doing down here?"

"I was restless and couldn't sleep so I came down."

"Are you mad at Daddy?"

"I'm not very happy about what he did. How's your face? Are you all right?"

"I'm okay." Amanda was sure her mother had come

downstairs because she'd had a fight with her father. She made herself a peanut-butter sandwich and took it upstairs with her and munched it in bed. But it was a long time before she could sleep.

Chapter Seven

❖❖❖❖❖❖❖❖❖❖❖❖❖❖❖❖❖❖❖❖❖❖❖❖❖❖❖❖❖❖❖❖

THE NEXT MORNING, SUNDAY, LISA WAS TRYING HER BEST to make conversation at the breakfast table. She chattered on about the play, she remarked on how good the pancakes were, but she couldn't get a rise out of anyone. Her mother and father weren't speaking to each other and Amanda just sat there looking glum.

"What's the matter with this family? No one will talk," she said finally.

"Why can't you be quiet?" Amanda snapped.

" 'Cause I don't feel like it. I'm going over to Fran's. This is boring."

Lisa got up and stalked out of the house. It was a glorious spring day and she tried to think of something exciting to do. When she got to Fran's house she suggested that they go for a walk.

"Where to?"

"Let's go to the park." There was a state park nearby that had good walking trails.

"It'll be muddy."

"Don't be so fussy," said Lisa. They walked to the park and found that it was muddy. Lisa wanted to keep on going, but Fran refused. "Come back to my house and we can play a game."

"I don't feel like doing that," Lisa scowled.

"What's the matter with you today? You're acting funny. Disagreeable."

"I don't know. I feel funny." She told Fran what Amanda had done the night before and that her parents had had a fight about it. "Swear you won't tell a soul. I feel weird talking about my family but I had to tell someone."

"I won't tell anybody. But gee, that was pretty terrific of Amanda. To go out like that."

"You think so?" Privately Lisa had been thinking the same thing herself. She could never openly defy anyone; she'd be afraid. Yet she didn't want to be like Amanda either. Amanda spent so much of her time being angry— mostly at their father but sometimes at a teacher or someone in school, and a lot of time at Lisa herself. Lisa hated quarrels. She wanted everything to be nice and smooth.

Even when her father wouldn't let her go down to the city to see Walter that time, she hadn't dreamed of kicking up a fuss about it, even though she was disappointed. Her mother once said that Lisa wanted everyone's approval, but Lisa couldn't see what was wrong with that. She did want everyone to like her, but today she felt different. She didn't know why.

"I'm going home," she said. "See you tomorrow."

"I thought you came over to do something with me." Fran looked disappointed and annoyed.

"I did, but I changed my mind. So long." Lisa walked home quickly. She had the queasy feeling that something was going on at home, something she shouldn't miss.

The house was ominously quiet when Lisa came in. Something *was* going on. She found her father sitting alone at the kitchen table with a cup of coffee in front of him. "Where's everybody? Where's Mom and Amanda?"

"They're upstairs." Her father avoided her eyes. There was an odd look on his face.

"What's the matter with this family? It's such a beautiful day and no one wants to go out."

Her father gave her a weak smile. "You don't have to stay in."

"I know."

Lisa went upstairs and into her mother's room. Her mother was lying on her bed and it was clear that she had been crying. "What's the matter?"

"Nothing. I guess I don't feel very well."

"You want anything?"

"No, dear. Just to be alone perhaps."

That was what her mother always said, especially when Lisa wanted to cuddle up and be near her. Feeling even more dissatisfied and uneasy, Lisa went into Amanda's room.

"How many times have I told you not to come in here without knocking?" Amanda said crossly, from her desk.

"Oh, shut up," Lisa snapped back.

Amanda looked up in surprise. "What's got into you?"

"Nothing. What's happening around here? Mom and Dad have another fight?"

"It's the same one. They go on and on."

"I wish they wouldn't."

A gleam of sympathy flickered in Amanda's eyes. "At least they don't fight about you as much as they do about me."

"It doesn't matter what they fight about," Lisa said, "it's horrible."

Both girls were silent as they heard their father come up the stairs and go into their parents' bedroom. There was the sound of subdued conversation, and then their mother's voice, loud and clear. "Don't be ridiculous, Mark. Do you really think you can come up here and make love and that will fix everything? Well, it doesn't work that way. I don't have push buttons that turn me on and off. And I don't find you very lovable at the moment."

"You rarely do anymore."

"Maybe. Please leave me alone."

" 'Leave me alone.' That's all you ever say. I'm sick of hearing it. You're too busy, you're too tired, I'm like an appendage in this household. All I do is pay the bills— God damn, I'm sick of being treated like some outsider . . ."

"And I'm sick of your setting the rules, your meting out punishments, your deciding what's right and what's wrong. First you act like a dictator, then you're sorry for yourself. Why don't you get wise and see what an ass you are?"

"I'll get wise. I'll get wise right now. You want to be alone, you can be alone. I'm getting out."

There was a dead silence for a few seconds. Then they heard their mother's voice, like ice. "If that's what you want to do then do it."

"It's what *you* want, isn't it? You've been building up to this."

"Don't put it on me," she yelled. "You go around like a sleepwalker. You don't pay any attention to me, you've no idea of what goes on in this house, you don't know anything about people's *feelings.*"

"If you find me such a monster, you're better off rid of me, aren't you? I'm sick of your putting me down every chance you get. You think you have all the answers, the perfect woman, you know all about how to bring up your daughters. So go ahead and do it, you don't need me."

Lisa went over and sat on Amanda's bed. Amanda

hoped that Lisa wasn't going to cry. It wasn't hard to figure out what was going on in their parents' room.

There was the sound of drawers being opened and
closed hastily. Then they heard their mother get up, go
downstairs and slam out of the house. A moment later her
car sped out of the driveway.

"Do you think they're both going to go away and leave
us alone? What'll we do, Amanda?" Lisa looked very
frightened.

"I don't think they'll do that. Mom'll be back. She
didn't take anything with her. Maybe Daddy's just pretending to leave. I don't think he really will." Amanda
wished she believed what she was telling Lisa.

"He's packing his clothes. Doesn't that mean he's leaving?"

"I don't know. Maybe he'll just go over to Grandma's
and then come back."

"I hope so."

But as they listened, he phoned a nearby hotel to re-
serve a room. When he came into Amanda's room, his face
was grim. It softened as he saw the way they were huddled
together on the bed. "I suppose you heard your mother
and me quarreling," he said. "This sometimes happens,
even when people care about each other. I've decided it
would be a good idea for us to have a cooling-off period—
get away from each other for a while. It's nothing permanent, and may not last long. I don't know. But for the
time being I'll be staying at the Fairfax. It's not far away

and I plan to see both of you a great deal. I'm not leaving you two—just a temporary separation from your mother."

"How can you leave her and not leave us?" asked Amanda. "We'll be here with her. If she's coming back. Is she?" Her eyes searched his face anxiously.

"I'm sure she is. I think she probably didn't want to be around while I was packing. None of this is fun for either of us. Or for you two either. It's not what I want . . ."

"Then why are you doing it?"

Her father smiled uneasily. "Sometimes we do things we don't like to do, but feel are necessary. I hope you kids will be a help to your mother. She'll need you."

"What about you?" Lisa asked. "Won't you mind being all alone?"

"I suppose I will. I'll miss you both very much. But I won't be that far away and I'll see a lot of you. And listen, you can call me any time—in the daytime you can get me at the office and in the evening at the hotel. Here's the number." He went over to Amanda's desk and wrote out the hotel phone number in large letters on a sheet of paper and left it on the desk blotter. "Call me whenever you want." Then he went back and kissed Amanda and took Lisa in his arms. "Be a good girl, baby."

Lisa nestled against his chest and started to cry. "I don't want you to go away. Why can't I come with you?"

"I think you're better off here. You wouldn't like living in a hotel."

"I wouldn't mind. Not if I could bring some of my

things with me. Please, Daddy, I really want to come with you."

Mark looked at her thoughtfully and wiped her cheeks with his handkerchief. "Well, we'll think about it. I'll talk to your mother. You stay here for now."

The girls followed him downstairs, and watched from the window as he threw his suitcase into his car and drove off. After he got out of the driveway he turned around and waved. Lisa sobbed loudly and ran up to her room. Amanda followed her upstairs more slowly. She couldn't believe what had happened—that her father had really left home. The more she thought about it, the worse she felt—as if it was all her fault. If she hadn't gone in the car with Randy it might never have happened. Better yet, if she hadn't been born her parents would have gotten along okay. They wouldn't have had fights about Lisa if she had been an only child.

As it grew dark Amanda began worrying about her mother. Maybe Lisa was right and they were going to be left alone. Amanda wondered if she should call their grandmother, but she didn't feel like having to talk to anyone. There was too much to explain.

Lisa lay on Amanda's bed crying, and Amanda sat down at her desk. She had a terrible headache and she didn't know what to do. She felt she should be taking care of Lisa but she didn't know how to get her to stop crying. She was just about ready to start crying herself.

Lisa startled her by jumping up from the bed suddenly and running to the window. "I hear Mommy's car."

Both girls ran down the stairs. Amanda was shocked by her mother's face; it was so sad and drawn. "Your father left, I suppose?"

The girls nodded and followed her into the kitchen where she put water on for tea. "Did he say anything to you?"

Amanda repeated Mark's words. Kate drew the two girls to her and encircled them with her arms. "We'll manage," she said with a weak smile. "I think it will all get straightened out. I hope you girls aren't going to be too upset. We both love you very much."

"It's all my fault," Amanda said. "You're always fighting about me."

Kate took Amanda's face between her hands. "You mustn't say that and you mustn't think that," she said. "You're not the problem. I know it sounds that way some of the time, but very often the things people seem to quarrel about are deceptive. Mark and I have different ideas and opinions about many things. We're both strong-minded and opinionated and we're bound to clash. But it's not about you, it's just that we're different. Sometimes those differences get out of hand and you have to do something drastic to break the pattern. I think that's what we're doing now. Having a cooling-off period. Maybe we'll all learn something."

"I don't want to learn anything," Lisa said. "I want Daddy. I don't want him to go away. Can I go stay with him?"

"You mean leave here?"

"Daddy said maybe I could. He said he'd talk to you."

Her mother's eyes filled with tears. "I don't suppose I could keep you if you really wanted to go. Let's think about it." She pulled Lisa close and gave her a hug. "I guess you are Daddy's girl, but I love you too."

"I know," Lisa said, but she wriggled out of her mother's arms. Suddenly she felt angry with her for quarreling so badly with her father.

Her mother let her go with an unhappy look. "Don't be angry with me, Lisa. We're both at fault, your father and me. Please don't blame just me."

"I'm not," Lisa lied. She left Amanda and her mother and went up to her room.

"Let her go with Daddy," Amanda said crossly, "if that's what she wants to do."

"We'll see," said her mother.

When the girls came home from school the next day, their mother was waiting for them. "How come you're not working?" asked Lisa.

"I wanted to be here when you got home."

"I hope you're not going to quit your job," Amanda said. "We can take care of ourselves. Daddy was never home in the afternoon anyway."

"I'm not quitting, don't worry. I know you girls can take care of yourselves. I felt like being home today, and besides I want to talk to you. Want something to eat?"

"No," Lisa said. "What do you want to talk about? Did you talk to Daddy?"

"Yes, I did. He'd like you to come and stay with him if you really want to, Lisa."

Lisa's eyes brightened. "I do, I do." Then her face fell. "But how would I get to school? The bus doesn't go over where he is."

"He said he'd make some arrangement. He can take you."

"But how would I get home?"

"I don't know. Your father will have to take care of that." Her mother was visibly irritated. "It's up to you whether you want to go or not. If you decide to go your father will have to work out the arrangements."

Lisa felt torn. She realized that her mother didn't want her to leave. But the thought of her father all alone in a hotel room was awful. And she had not gotten over her feeling of resentment against her mother—if her mother had really wanted to, she could have kept her father from leaving. They were both looking at her, waiting for her answer. Once again it seemed as if they were on one side and she was on the other.

"I'll go," she said. She turned away as she saw her mother's eyes fill with tears. "Amanda, will you take care of my cat?"

Amanda nodded yes.

"I'll help you put some things together," her mother said shakily. Then she ran out of the room and the girls heard her close the door of the bathroom.

"She's crying."

"It's not my fault," Lisa said defensively. She didn't like the look in Amanda's eyes.

"Whose fault is it? Of course it's your fault. Yours and Daddy's. You only care about yourselves. I'm glad you're going with him."

"You're mean. You're the meanest person I ever knew. I hope all your hair falls out." Lisa was about to storm out of the kitchen when Kate reappeared.

"Girls, *please*. I can't stand any more fighting. Don't you two start. Haven't we had enough of this? Come on, Lisa, let's get you packed. I called Mark, he's coming to pick you up from work."

Lisa followed her mother up the stairs and Amanda called out that she was going over to see their grandmother.

Chapter Eight

❖◆❖◆❖◆❖◆❖◆❖◆❖◆❖◆❖◆❖◆❖◆❖◆❖◆❖◆❖◆❖◆❖◆❖◆❖

"I SUPPOSE YOU KNOW WHAT HAPPENED," AMANDA SAID, settling herself against the pillows of Margo's sofa.

"Yes, I do. I've been terribly upset. How's your mother?"

"Crying. Lisa's going over to live with Daddy."

"Oh, no," said Margo. "I wish she wasn't doing that."

"Why?" asked Amanda. "Aren't you glad he won't be alone?"

"He might come home faster if he were alone. This whole thing is ridiculous," Margo said angrily. "Two civilized people—you'd think they wouldn't be so—so *petty*. It isn't as if they had any major differences. They've just forgotten how to be polite to each other—not manners polite, but the real meaning of the word, *considerate.*"

"Do you think Daddy will come home?"

"I think so, I hope so. But I don't know, Amanda. I just don't know."

Margo's uncertainty was too painful. Amanda changed the subject.

"Are you going to marry Mr. Adams?"

"I think I may. I like him very much."

"Then you wouldn't be alone anymore."

"I don't mind being alone. I wouldn't marry anyone out of loneliness; I'd have to have a better reason than that. To like him a lot."

"But it doesn't make any difference, does it? I mean my parents must have liked each other when they got married, didn't they?"

"I'm sure they did."

"But they don't anymore. Like each other, I mean. Getting married seems stupid."

"That's not so. It can be pretty wonderful. Your parents have had a lot of happy times together, and I think they will again. But if it doesn't work out they'll still have had the good times—no one can take those away."

"I think they've forgotten the good times," Amanda said. "Are you going to stay friends with Mommy?"

"Of course, darling. What a question! I love your mother, she's like a daughter to me."

"Grandparents sometimes take sides. A kid in school never sees her father's parents anymore, not since her mother and father got divorced."

"Your parents aren't divorced yet. Anyway, that would be ridiculous. Don't worry. You'll see more of me than ever."

"Will Lisa too?"

"Of course. I expect I'll see you together. You and Lisa will be seeing each other. I'm sure you'll want to."

"Maybe," Amanda said dubiously. "I'd better be going home to Mommy." Amanda got up and kissed her grandmother goodbye. "I hope she's stopped crying."

Although it was the third morning Lisa had woken up in her hotel room, she still didn't know where she was when she opened her eyes. Everything looked strange— the ugly pink-and-yellow-flowered wallpaper, the nondescript chest of drawers, and the imitation Van Goghs on the wall. "The worst reproductions," her father had commented.

Mornings were the hardest. Each morning Lisa had to remind herself that her parents were separated, that she was living in a hotel bedroom and that in truth for the time being she had no home at all. Her father, who was in the room next door, had said he wouldn't be hurt if she went home. Her mother had told her it would make her very happy if she came back, and her grandmother had said she shouldn't be ashamed to change her mind. Even

Amanda had mumbled something to the effect that she had been dumb to leave.

Yet Lisa felt compelled to stay, although she couldn't really explain why to anyone. It was a combination of many reasons: she felt her father needed her and to leave would be deserting him. He looked so sad these days. And to go home would be to forgive her mother, something Lisa wasn't quite ready to do yet. Lisa still believed her mother was to blame, because she hadn't asked her father not to go. If she had, her father wouldn't have left—Lisa was positive. As for changing her mind, Lisa felt to do so would be a kind of defeat. Taking a stand with her father made her feel independent in a way she never had before. In fact, every day that she could get along without Amanda and without her mother made her feel stronger.

Once Lisa was wide awake she jumped out of bed happier than she had been since she left home. Tonight she was going home to have dinner with her mother and Amanda. She could barely wait. In spite of her determination not to give up and go home, she did miss her mother and her sister—very much, really. If only everyone would get together again, Lisa thought as she got dressed, she wouldn't be going through all these strange up and down feelings.

She was ready when her father knocked on her door. Together they went down to the coffee shop for breakfast. Lisa had imagined it would be fun to eat her meals in restaurants, but she was already tired of the menu. No matter how she asked for her eggs, they always came the same, with the white too soft and runny. She hated them that way. And the bacon wasn't nice and crisp the way her mother made it.

"What time do you want me to pick you up tonight?"

"I don't know. Can I stay till eleven?"

"Better make it ten, it's a school night."

Lisa was so glad he didn't say nine that she didn't argue. "Daddy, are you going to look for an apartment? I'm tired of this hotel."

"So soon?" He smiled. "You can go home, you know."

"I know. But I don't want to. You said you'd find an apartment."

"I've thought about it. I don't think it's a good idea, not yet. It makes everything too permanent. Your mother and I have a lot of things to talk over first."

"You mean about getting back together?"

"Yes. I think it's better to stay here. Try to be patient, honey."

"Okay." Her father was talking to her as if she were an adult and she liked that. She hoped that her mother and Amanda would notice how grown up she had become in just a few days. They had better not treat her like a baby.

The day dragged for Lisa, but by three o'clock she was happy and excited to get on her regular bus home with Amanda. The other days she had had to take a public interurban bus that let her out near the hotel.

When they arrived, Kate was putting juice and cookies on the kitchen table. There were tears in her eyes when she hugged Lisa. "We're having a party," Lisa said, when the three of them sat down.

"She's only been gone three days," Amanda said. "What's all the fuss about?"

"There's no fuss," her mother said. "You always like something when you come home from school."

"It's funny visiting my own house," said Lisa. She pushed the plate of cookies away from her abruptly, saying, "I feel funny, Mommy."

"Do you want to go to the bathroom?" Lisa's face had turned pale.

She nodded, and ran from the room. Kate followed her hurriedly. Lisa just managed to get to the bathroom before she was sick. "I wanted to show you how grown up I was," she sobbed. "I don't know what happened, it came on so fast . . ."

"It's nerves, darling. You've been under a strain, we all have. As you said, to come here to visit is very strange. It's hard . . ."

Lisa sat on the edge of the bathtub and her mother wiped her face with a cool cloth. "I don't like it. Mommy, will you ask Daddy to come back?"

Her mother sighed. "It's not so simple. People say things they're sorry for, and then they get into situations they don't know how to get out of."

Lisa washed her face and combed her hair but she still

didn't feel right. All through the rest of the afternoon Amanda and her mother talked about things that had happened while she had been away. They laughed about a prowler they'd heard the night before. He'd turned out to be the boy next door, looking for something on the ground in the dark. Hearing this, Lisa felt a familiar irritation, the same old sense of being excluded, and wondered why she'd been so excited about coming home. But a few minutes later, when she was describing all her restaurant meals, she felt hopeful again, particularly when her mother asked several times how Daddy was. "I hope he's not working too hard," she said, with real concern in her voice.

By early evening, Lisa felt exhausted by her somersaulting emotions. She cuddled up close to her mother and gave a sigh of relief when she felt her mother's warm, strong arms around her. She couldn't help it—she wanted to be a baby and grown up all at once. She wanted her family to be together, and for *both* her parents to love her the same.

After supper they all watched television, and for a while Lisa could pretend that nothing had changed, that it was an ordinary night and their father was out on business. But the illusion was shattered when he arrived at ten o'clock to pick her up. Lisa was watchful as he kissed Kate on the cheek and she responded with a small hug and a smile. If they were so mad at each other, why were they kissing?

She asked Amanda when they were alone together, packing up some of Lisa's clothes. "I guess they're not mad all the time. Besides, married people like to kiss. Anyway, I'm glad. I wish he'd come home soon."

"You do? I thought you didn't like him."

"Don't be silly. He's my father, isn't he? Sometimes he gets me mad, but I guess he can't help it. Mom says he doesn't mean to put me down. He's a perfectionist and he expects everyone else to be one too."

"Will you be glad if I come back?"

Amanda considered the question. "I wouldn't mind," she offered cautiously. Seeing the anxiety in Lisa's face she added, "Sure—it's boring here alone. Besides, your cat misses you, so you'd better come back." She grinned.

Lisa was pleased. She could tell that Amanda really did miss her a little.

Their parents were sitting in the kitchen talking earnestly, but they stopped when Lisa and Amanda came in.

Lisa felt very strange kissing her mother goodbye and then giving Amanda an awkward kiss goodnight. She ran out to her father's car ahead of him, glad it was dark so he wouldn't see she was crying.

Chapter Nine

❖•❖

"I HATE SUNDAYS," SAID AMANDA.

"You used to like them." Barbara looked up from the social studies book she was reading on Amanda's floor.

"I know, but it's different now. If I spend it with Daddy and Lisa, Mommy looks sad and mopey, and if I stay home *I* feel sad and mopey. It's awful. I wish they'd decide what they're going to do—it's been a month since they left. I hate not knowing."

"I wonder what will make them decide. I hope when I grow up I won't have to get divorced."

"I know I won't because I'm never getting married."

"How do you know? You're too young. You may fall in love with someone and want to get married." Barbara giggled. "Like Randy."

"I'm never going to fall in love with anyone. What's the sense? You get all mixed up and you're miserable."

"Everyone isn't. Some people are happy."

"They'd be happy anyway. Darn it, I wish my father was here to help me with my math."

"I do too. Then you could show me. I hate math."

"I do too." Amanda chewed on her pencil thoughtfully. "You know, that's not really true. Swear you won't laugh at me?"

Barbara nodded.

"I really like math. I just keep saying I hate it to bug my father—because he bugs me about it. I don't want to give him the satisfaction of saying I like it. That's stupid, isn't it?"

"I don't know. Do you *like* to fight with your father?"

"Sometimes I do. Sometimes I just want to cry, but other times—I don't know, it's like winning a game. He's very smart, so if I come out even I feel I've done something."

"Maybe that's why you tell him you hate math, just to fight. Sometimes I do that with my parents. If my mother tells me to wear something, even if I meant to wear it all along, I decide to wear something else. It gets her so mad."

"I know. But who wants to be told what to do all the

time? If they left us alone we'd get along better."

"I know. If I ever have kids I'm never going to nag them."

Amanda jumped up from her desk. "I've got an idea. I'm going to call my father. He said I could call him any time I wanted. I'm going to ask him if I can see him to-night. Then he can help me with my math. Do you think he'll do it?" She started to chew on her pencil nervously.

"I don't know. It depends. Sometimes my father likes to help me, but not if he's watching a ball game on TV. Then he doesn't even want me to talk to him."

"My father doesn't always watch the games. I'm going to try."

Amanda went into her mother's room to use the phone. She came back beaming. "He's going to take me out for dinner. It's perfect because Lisa is staying overnight with Fran so she won't have to come with us."

Barbara left soon to go home, and Amanda took a shower and washed her hair. Feeling pleased and excited about her decision to see her father, she put on her favorite blouse and skirt and her new black sandals.

She was waiting for him to pick her up when her mother came home from work. "Where are you going?" she asked.

"Out for dinner with Daddy."

Her mother put her bags of groceries down on the kitchen counter. "When did you decide that? I brought all this stuff home for supper."

"I called him. I want him to help me with my math."

"You could have called me at the office. This is very inconsiderate."

"I'm sorry, Mom. I didn't think of it."

"No, of course not," she said, annoyed. "No one thinks of anyone in this family."

"What family?" Amanda snapped.

"Oh, boy, that hurts. What family! We're still a family, Amanda . . ." Her mother's eyes filled with tears and she wiped them away with the back of her hand. "It seems I'm always crying these days. We're all hurting, Amanda . . . we're all hurt and angry and we keep taking it out on each other. It's got to come to an end soon, we can't go on like this."

"Poor Mom, I'm really sorry. It's awful, isn't it? It's worse for you . . ." She put her arms around Kate.

"Don't 'poor Mom' me, please, I can't stand it. I can take care of myself, it's not that . . . I love Mark. We fight and we have differences, but that doesn't keep me from loving him. If we could only respect our differences we'd be all right."

Well, why can't you, then? Amanda thought, and then wondered if she could ever respect Lisa's differences. "Do you mean like Lisa and me?" she asked.

Her mother nodded.

"But the way she acts bothers me so much sometimes. Like when she gets so cute and silly. How can I respect that?"

"Maybe it's a question of just trying to accept it," her

mother said. "Not rejecting it because it's different from the way you want it to be. Does that make sense?"

"I think so." At that moment Amanda heard her father's car horn. She kissed her mother goodbye and ran out to meet him.

In the car, Amanda felt shy with her father, as she had every time she'd seen him this month. It was queer to answer all his questions about school and her mother slowly and politely, as if they were strangers instead of father and daughter. At least when they argued they had been communicating something real. Their conversation now seemed so beside the point. Still, Amanda answered him dutifully. "School's okay. Mom and I get along fine. I don't do much in the afternoons—I usually see Barbara."

When they got to the restaurant Amanda asked, "Can I have lobster?"

"Have anything you want," her father said. "Shoot the works."

Amanda ordered lobster and french fries and a Caesar salad, her favorite. "Are you rich?" she asked.

He smiled. "No, I'm a member of the great middle class. I'll never be rich, but we won't go hungry. Why do you ask?"

"I was thinking that if you and Mommy stay apart you and Lisa will be richer than Mommy and me. You make more money than she does, don't you?"

"I guess I do. But she doesn't work full-time. Are you worried about our staying apart?"

"Yes. I don't like things being up in the air. I'd like to

know if my parents are going to be divorced or not."

"Is that what you wanted to talk about when you called me?" Her father sipped his wine and Amanda drank her tomato juice.

"Not really." Amanda wriggled uncomfortably in her chair. "I called you because I need help with my math."

He laughed. "At least you're honest. I'm glad I'm good for something. Is that all you need me for?"

"No, of course not." She gave him a level gaze. "But you are critical of me. I don't seem to ever do anything right for you." Amanda started in on her lobster.

"I think you're exaggerating. I do expect a lot from you, but you don't understand why. You have an exceptionally good mind and I want to see you use it. What you call criticizing I call having high expectations."

"But you don't do that to Lisa. You let her get away with a lot."

"Maybe. But I don't expect the same of her. Lisa has a good mind, but it's different from yours; it's intuitive. You have an analytical mind. You can learn to grasp abstract theories. Not everyone can do that—it's a real talent."

Amanda realized that her father was giving her a big compliment. She felt pleased and a little embarrassed. "You don't usually say nice things to me."

Her father laughed but he was serious when he answered. "You don't hear them. Did it ever occur to you that you take everything I say as a put-down?"

"No."

"Think about it."

"Okay."

When they finished dinner they went back to the hotel and sat down to work on Amanda's math. She did the problems by herself and when she was finished she gave him her paper to look over.

He crossed out the first one he looked at with his pen. Amanda was indignant. "Now you've spoiled the whole paper! Besides, what's wrong with that problem? I did it the way you told me to."

"You did not. You weren't listening. You can't add 'a' and 'b'; it makes no sense. First you have to figure out how many miles were walked. You weren't thinking. You just went ahead in a hurry. Careless and sloppy."

"Don't call me careless and sloppy," Amanda yelled. "Just because I did one problem wrong doesn't make me careless and sloppy. You haven't even looked at the others! And you didn't have to mark it with your pen. Now I have to do the whole page over! Don't even look at the rest." She snatched the paper out of his hand.

"Don't shout at me. What if you do have to do the page over? The important thing is to get it right. Don't you have any pride in your work? To have it be right and look right?"

"I don't care how it looks. This is math, not a beauty contest."

"Damn it, you should care about what you do. How do you think a client of mine would like it if I handed in a set of plans crossed out and inked over? I wouldn't be in business very long."

"That's different." Amanda turned away in despair. "We just can't get along. You say I've got a mind, but you're always calling me stupid . . ."

"I didn't say stupid, I said careless. They're not the same. Carelessness you can do something about."

"Maybe I don't want to do anything about it. I'm never going to be anything, anyway. You've told me that a million times." She gathered up her papers and math book.

"What are you doing? Don't you want to finish?"

"What's the sense? We'll only fight more."

"Hey, wait a minute." Her father got up and put his arm around her. "You came over here to get help, didn't you? So let's do the math." He led her back to her chair and sat down next to her. But he didn't pick up the math papers. Instead he lit his pipe and looked at Amanda with serious eyes. "Your mother says we both have short fuses, and she's right. But if we just remember that we love each other our anger won't hurt us."

"It does hurt, though. I hate it when you make me feel so stupid. I want to hit back." Amanda wiped her tear-stained face with a tissue.

"I'm sorry I'm so short-tempered, but it's because I expect so much of you. I shouldn't impose my expectations on you, I know it's not fair. But the fact is I do and we'll both have to live with it. I'm forty years old and I don't think I can change much."

"I guess I wouldn't mind your getting mad at me once in a while if you said nice things to me too." Amanda smoothed her crumpled math paper and held it out to her father. "Do you want to look at the rest of these?"

"Of course," he said. He leaned over and gave her a hug. "You're a wonderful girl, Amanda," he said. "I'm glad you're my daughter."

When she got home that night Amanda sat down to write in her journal.

I think my father really does care about me. I'm going to stop being jealous of Lisa (not right away, but little by little). She's pretty and cute, but I am going to be an interesting woman. I think that's more important because you can stay being that way even when you get to be forty years old and have wrinkles. I hope my parents don't get divorced because I miss Daddy very much. I miss Lisa too even if sometimes she is a pest.

Chapter Ten

❖❖❖❖❖❖❖❖❖❖❖❖❖❖❖❖❖❖❖❖❖❖❖❖❖❖❖❖❖❖

SEVERAL DAYS LATER LISA SAT IN HER ROOM WAITING
for her father to come back to the hotel. She was thinking
about how lonesome she was when the phone rang. "He's
not home yet," she said to her sister. "You want him to
call you when he gets here?"

"Okay."

"What are you and Mommy doing tonight?"

"Nothing. Just staying home."

"What are you having for supper?"

"Leftover chicken, I guess. Unless Mommy brings
something else home."

"Oh. That sounds nice. I'm so tired of eating in restaurants," Lisa confessed.

"Why don't you move back home?" Amanda hadn't planned on saying that, but as soon as she did she was glad.

"I've been thinking about it. But ... do you think it would be mean to Daddy?"

"No, he'd understand. And maybe he'd come too."

"I wish he would. I'm sick of living this way."

"Me too. It's so quiet around here. And I think Mom misses you and Daddy a whole lot. And ... I do too," she added, a little awkwardly.

"Thanks," said Lisa, feeling pleased. "I miss you too," she offered. "And I guess it's okay if you and Mom have secrets *sometimes.*"

Amanda laughed. "Call us back after you talk to him, okay?"

"Sure."

Lisa could hardly wait for her father to come home. When he did arrive she had to wait while he took a shower and changed into his casual clothes. As soon as he opened a can of beer and sat down to read the paper Lisa said she wanted to talk to him.

"Okay. What's on your mind?"

"Daddy, can I go home?"

He looked at her with some surprise. "Are you so miserable here, baby?"

Lisa shook her head vigorously. "No, it's not that. I don't know ... I guess I'm homesick." She went over to him and put her arms around him. "Would you mind very much?"

Her father kissed her on the cheek. "I'd miss you, but by all means go. Does your mother know?"

"No, I just told Amanda that I was thinking about it."

"When do you want to go?"

Lisa hugged him. "Tonight? It wouldn't take me long to pack."

Her father laughed. "You're not wasting any time, are you? I think you'd better talk to your mother first, just to make sure she'll be home."

Lisa hesitated before going to the phone. She didn't want to hurt him. "You won't be too lonesome, will you?"

"I'll cry every night," he said teasingly. "Go ahead, get it over with." He walked over to the window and stood with his back to her while she made the call. Lisa was afraid he might be upset; Kate, too, was concerned about Mark. "You're sure he'll be all right? He doesn't mind too much?"

"He says it's okay. Can I come?"

"Of course! I'm very happy. Amanda will be too. And Grandma will be here tonight—she'll be so glad to see you."

"Save some supper for me."

"We'll wait."

Lisa was bubbling with excitement as she packed her clothes. "I'll come visit you and have dinners with you the same as Amanda does. If we came on different nights you'd hardly ever have to eat alone. Isn't that a good idea?"

"That'll be just fine," her father agreed.

Soon she was ready to leave and he took her over in the car. "Are you coming in?" Lisa asked when he pulled into the driveway.

"Of course. Don't you want me to?"

"Yes, I do. I wish you were living here again, Daddy."

"We'll see," was all he said.

Inside the house, Mark kissed Amanda and his mother and then Kate. Seeing her parents together made Lisa wonder if they weren't just being silly about not making up. Like the times when she got mad at Amanda and then felt sorry but didn't know how to say so.

Kate asked Mark if he wanted to stay for supper, but he seemed uncomfortable and said that he had to go back to his office to do some work. As soon as he left Lisa ran up to her room. Her cat was on the bed and she lay down next to her and took her in her arms. "I'm not going to leave you ever again," she said softly. "Ever, ever." Her eyes roamed the room resting on each of her favorite objects: the big poster of two yellow cats, the red-and-gold mobile swaying over her desk, the panda sitting on the bookshelf and the snapshots of her mother and father stuck in the bureau mirror. It was so good to be home.

Lisa settled down at her usual place at the supper table with a happy grin on her face. "If Daddy was here everything would be normal."

Amanda gave her a warning look while Kate served the food. "Did you eat lobster every night?" Amanda asked.

"No, I hate lobster."

"You'd probably rather go to McDonald's," said her grandmother.

"Sometimes. Most of the time Daddy took me to nice restaurants. But I like Mommy's cooking."

"I'm glad you do. Thank you. It's nice to have you here."

"It's nice to be here," Lisa said. "I'm glad this isn't just a visit."

When they were eating dessert Margo said, "I have an announcement."

"I bet I know what it is," said Kate, looking pleased. "But I'll let you tell it."

Margo had a wide smile on her face. "Michael and I are going to be married."

In seconds the two girls and Kate were kissing and hugging her. "I'm so happy," Kate said. "He's a lovely man and he's very lucky to get you."

"I'm lucky too," Margo said.

"When is it going to be?" asked Amanda.

"Can I be a bridesmaid?" Lisa gave her grandmother another hug.

"We haven't set a date yet, but it will be soon. And I don't expect I'll have bridesmaids. It's going to be very simple. Maybe Kate and Mark will stand up with us. How would you feel about that?" she asked Kate.

"You know I'd love it. I'm sure Mark will be very pleased."

"I hope so. I just wish . . ." her voice trailed off.

"I know what you're thinking," Kate said. "I guess we all wish it were different."

"You mean that you and Daddy were together again?" Amanda asked. "I don't see why you're not. I think this is stupid."

"Maybe it is, but parents can't always run their lives for their children. Sometimes they have to think of themselves." Kate's voice was sharp.

"I know they do," Amanda said, giving her mother an unhappy glance.

"I want to be *something* at your wedding," Lisa said. "You're my only grandmother."

"We'll see what we can do," Margo promised.

Late that night Lisa crossed the hall to Amanda's room. "What's the matter?" asked Amanda as Lisa sat down on the bed.

"I can't sleep."

Amanda groaned. "Tomorrow's school. And I'm really tired."

"Can't I just sit here for a little while?"

"Okay." She sat up. "What's the matter, are you sorry you came home?"

Lisa began to cry. "No, but I'm scared Mommy and Daddy will get divorced. Everything was so nice before."

"Are you kidding? We fought all the time, Lisa."

"Well, so what if we had some arguments? No one really meant them."

"I don't know about that."

"You don't hate me just because we fight, do you?"

"Sometimes."

"But then you get over it, right? And we're sort of friends again."

"I guess so." Lisa's directness surprised her. "But anyway," said Amanda, "it's not up to us. It's up to Mommy and Daddy to decide."

"I think we should have a vote. We're in this family as much as they are. It's not fair for two people to decide what happens to four people."

"It isn't fair, but we can't do much about it." Amanda yawned.

"We can try not to take sides all the time," persisted Lisa. "That would help."

"Okay, okay," said Amanda. "But that means you can't always cuddle up to Daddy to get your way."

"Well, I won't do that if you promise not to have so many secrets with Mommy. Sometimes I feel like she's not interested in me at all," Lisa added.

"That's not true." Amanda felt a pang of guilt. Maybe she should try not to take up all of her mother's free time. "Anyway, it's a deal." She yawned again. "Now can I go to sleep?"

"Shake on it." Lisa stuck a pudgy hand out in the dark.

"Boy, you're really something," said Amanda. But she shook on it, just the same.

On the sunny June day of Margo's wedding, Kate was as excited as her daughters. "I love having the wedding party here," she said as she divided up the flowers to be arranged in vases, and gave a bunch to each of the girls. "I hope you two get married at home."

"*If* we get married," Amanda said.

A few minutes later she and Lisa ran upstairs to put on their new dresses. Soon they were ready to go to the church with their mother. Mark was already there when they arrived. He was going to give his mother away to her groom.

The ceremony was brief and solemn. Lisa stood close to Amanda and had to control her giggles when Michael fumbled with the ring and nearly dropped it. Everyone kissed the bride when it was over, and suddenly their mother burst into tears. The girls saw Mark go to her quickly, put his arms around her and hold her while she cried against his shoulder. They watched silently as their parents drew away from the others and sat down in an empty pew to talk. Neither one of them missed the fact that Mark was holding both of Kate's hands in his.

Lisa took hold of Amanda's hand and held it tight. "Do you think?" she whispered.

"Sh-sh. Don't say anything. You'll spoil it."

Lisa nodded. She understood.

Back at their house, Kate's face was unusually flushed and Mark wore a slightly foolish grin on his face as he helped her to set out the food. Amanda thought he was making rather a big thing out of helping; she knew her mother preferred to do that sort of job herself. But Kate seemed to enjoy his awkward attempts, even though they did slow things down and the guests began to arrive before they were quite finished.

For a while Amanda and Lisa were kept busy greeting people, passing plates and helping to take empty glasses back into the kitchen. Later on, when everyone gathered to watch Margo and Michael cut the wedding cake, the girls stood close to their parents, and both noticed at the same time that their father had his arm around their mother's waist.

A bit later Margo and Michael started saying their goodbyes before leaving on a brief honeymoon. Amanda and Lisa hugged their grandmother hard.

"We're going to see each other as much as ever," Margo whispered, wiping away a few tears. "I promise you."

Amanda couldn't answer, but she gave her grandmother a powerful hug.

It was dusk before the last guest left. Kate stretched out on the living room sofa and kicked off her shoes. "It was a beautiful wedding but I'm exhausted."

"The girls and I will clean up. You rest," said Mark.

"You don't have to. Mrs. Jenkins is coming back with her daughter. She just went home to get out of her finery."

"Then should I . . . ?"

Kate nodded. "Sure, why not?"

Mark sat down and smiled at Lisa and Amanda. "Your

mother and I have something we want to say to you . . ." He looked at Kate for support.

"Go ahead. You tell them," she said.

"Okay. What I want to say is that I'm coming home. I hope . . ." His words were cut short as Lisa threw her arms around him. "Oh, I'm so happy . . . I knew it. I could tell . . . oh, Daddy, I'm so glad . . ." Mark hugged her and then looked over her head at Amanda. "How do you feel about it?"

Amanda was smiling but her eyes were serious. "It's great. I'm glad. You never should have left."

He laughed. "You sound more like my mother than my daughter." Turning to Kate, he said, "I'll go back and get my things and check out of the hotel. Okay?"

"Of course. Don't be long."

"Can I come with you?" asked Lisa.

Mark hesitated. "No, you stay here. I'll be back soon."

"But I want to come."

"I'd rather go alone. Don't pout, Lisa, you're getting too big for that." Mark gave his wife a kiss goodbye and went out.

Lisa picked up a cushion and threw it. "Why wouldn't he let me go with him?"

"He wanted to go alone," said her mother.

"He's telling you not to be a baby anymore," Amanda said shrewdly. "That you can't get your own way with him all the time."

"I don't care," Lisa said defiantly, but she picked up

the cushion and put it back on the sofa.

Later that evening after Mark had come home, the family sat in the living room watching television. Lisa was cuddled up next to her father, Amanda was on the floor, and Kate was back in her favorite position on the sofa. The program they had been watching together was finished, and Amanda got up and switched to another channel.

"Why'd you do that? I want to watch the news," said her father.

"But my show is on here. I watch it every Saturday night." Amanda turned up the volume.

"Turn that thing off," he said with irritation. "It's time for you to go to bed anyway." He got up and switched back to the station he wanted.

"Mommy let me watch it when you weren't here. Change it back!" she demanded.

Her father looked so angry Amanda thought he was going to slap her. They stood facing each other silently; then he ran his hand through his hair and stepped back. Amanda's throat choked with sobs. "Nothing's changed. Nothing. You're just as mean as ever," she cried.

Her father took hold of her shoulders as if by sheer force he could stop her sobbing and shaking. "Amanda, be quiet," he said softly. He put his arms around her and held her until she quieted down. Then he led her to his big armchair, sat down, and gestured for her to sit too. But she simply stood there, cold and rigid.

"Sit down, Amanda," her mother said. "Your father wants to talk to you."

Amanda looked at her mother, surprised at the unfamiliar note of firmness in her voice, and sat down.

"You are right," her father said. "Nothing tremendous has changed. We're the same people—each of us. We have the same faults and the same virtues we had before. But if every one of us hasn't learned a lesson by the recent upheaval in this family we're pretty stupid, and I don't think we are. We're bound to disagree, and fight and get mad—it's all part of loving and intimacy, living in one house together. But we've *got* to make accommodations, every one of us. We can't each have our own way. You understand?"

"I suppose so," Amanda said. "But what if I forget?"

He laughed. "I'll be here to remind you."

"I will too. I'll remember," Lisa offered.

"You stay out of it," Amanda said. "This is between Daddy and me."

"No, it's not," Mark said. "This goes for all of us, and we're not going to have this lining up of sides either. We're a family of four, not two and two."

"Except when we play a game," Lisa said practically. "And we have to choose partners."

"That's right," Kate said when they stopped laughing, "only when we play a game."